SACRILEGE

Barbara Avon

SACRILEGE

Written by Barbara Avon

Twitter: @barb_avon

Cover Design by Barbara Avon

Acknowledgements

They are only words that are strung together and meant to elicit an emotional response in the reader. To an author, words are everything. This is the part where I am able to express my gratitude with two simple words that hold so much meaning. Thank you to Scott Christopher Beebe, Author; Morgan Wright, Author; Daniel Lacho of Guru Art Lifestyle Entertainment; Jacqueline Belle, Author; Peter Talley, Author; and friends Lacy Gordon, Aaron Gould, and David Strover. Your kindness resides in my heart.

Words of love go to my family. Without them, I would be someone else entirely, and that, to me, is unimaginable.

I would like to acknowledge my incredible husband. When we met, he was a man of few words; turns out, he was hoarding them. Each one is precious, forever cherished. Thank you -- for everything.

I am indebted to my readers. Without them, I would still write, but it is because of them, that I am unstoppable.

"Sacrilege" is primarily meant to entertain all those who delve headfirst into the eerie, and mysterious side of life. It's also a love story between an unlikely pair who eventually find solace in one another; two imperfect souls who tumble into darkness. This is their story.

Please note that there are dark and sensitive themes throughout this story.

"You hear the whistle?

As the train draws near, I can hear a miscreant pleading for absolution. He's surrendering to the demon conductor who is taking him home. Their journey, infinite. 'All aboard', he's crying."

"The demon?"

"The miscreant."

"Disguised beneath a delicate shell, is the monster I call 'woman.'"

-Cris Corelli's Diary, October 10th, 1985

One

The boarding house façade was weathered by years of neglect, made worse by pigeon excrement that dripped down the red brick like the tears too often spent by the righteous souls who slumbered within. Its peaks rivaled the breasts he recently suckled during a brief, lewd affair in a train depot stall.

Cristoforo Corelli scratched at his naked neck. He had ditched the sacred collar by the side of the road on a drunken walk home from *Herley's Bar,* thrusting a symbolic middle finger towards God. That night, cloaked in darkness, he had pulled it from his jeans and beneath a smattering of rain, he tossed it into a water-filed ditch and watched the pristine white transition into the same colour as his blackened heart. At home, accompanied by the roaches, he indulged in the last nightcap he would ever consume, washing away remnants of his former life with swigs of Holy wine. He left what little he possessed on the Formica, save for the likeness of his mother housed in a simple frame, his *Hollies'* collection on Cassette tape, and his well-read Bible that served to remind him of that for which he was to atone. Unlike the man who takes his own life, Corelli skipped the formality of a letter, and boarded the midnight train to an unknown destination intent to shed the skin that felt taut against his asphyxiated soul.

At the top of the stairs, he examined the etchings in the wood of the massive door; signatures left by those seeking sanctuary and being denied entry. The heavy brass knocker was unadorned, and he lifted it and dropped it, once. He was acutely aware of the hour when the door opened, introducing him to a young woman dressed in red shorts and a black tank top. Her legwarmers were nestled against her calves. Her dark hair matched his own and was piled messily atop her head. Her demeanor lacked finesse when she opened her mouth to speak the words meant to dissuade the lone traveler.

"It's late."

"I know. I need a room."

She scrutinized the man who bore a resemblance to her father in black and white pictures of him in his army greens before a bullet dispersed his brains over foreign soil.

"Do you have money?"

"I have enough."

She stepped away, pulling the door fully open, inviting him into the foyer that was plastered with signs advertising Boarding House policy, and one misspelled sign that made him cringe: *Me Casa, es su Casa.*

"Thanks," Corelli said, dropping his backpack to his feet.

"How long are you staying?" the woman asked, securing the door for the night.

"As long as it takes. What's your name?"

"What does it matter?"

"I'll just refer to you as 'woman', then," he said, dispassionately.

"Jules."

"As in rubies, and shit?"

"As in 'July'. Do you want a room, or not?"

Leaving his backpack on the floor, Corelli walked towards the threshold of the adjoining room, an expansive space with long tables set up in the fashion of a Bingo Hall.

"How much?" he asked the woman without facing her.

She walked to stand before him, adopting a stance she reserved for Bill Collectors, and rowdy guests.

"Fifty a week. Eighty if you want meals, too. Breakfast ends at eight. If you like to sleep, you don't eat. I need half as deposit. No refunds."

Corelli shrugged off his black leather jacket and reached into the inner pocket producing a money clip.

"My grandpa had one just like it," Jules said, mocking him.

Ignoring her, he counted out sixteen ten-dollar bills and handed them to his new host. "That's two weeks. Paid in full."

"I can count," she said, flipping through the stack. She stuffed the cash in her bra, opting out of writing a receipt. "Follow me."

Corelli threw his jacket back on, retrieved his backpack from the foyer, and followed the woman to an office riddled with hundreds of leather-bound antique books that seemed misplaced in a world where rock music was coveted, and poets went ignored. His fingers traced the page of one opened book at the side of the large, oak desk where, behind it, Jules busied herself with the House ledger.

Man comes and tills the field and lies, beneath,
And after many a summer dies the swan.
Me and cruel immortality
Consumes: I wither slowly in thine arms...

"Tennyson."

"Yours?"

"What of it?" she asked, raising her head from her work.

"Are you always this warm?"

"It's two in the fucking morning, and you came to me, remember? Sign here. Add the date and time," she said, turning a book in his direction.

Corelli signed his name like a million times before, scratched out the moniker "Father" and tried again, noting the time as 2:01 A.M. He watched as Jules opened a drawer, withdrew a cash box, and deposited the bills.

"That's a big eating area," he said, gesturing behind him. "How many rooms do you have?"

"Only three. We rent that space out to the locals for meetings and things like that. Extra cash."

"Got it."

"Here's your key," she told him, handing him something on a string. "Don't lose it. You're at the top of the stairs. The only open door. You'll find linen and towels in the dresser. No visitors allowed without informing me first. Any questions…Cris?" she asked, glancing at the ledger.

"Who is 'we'?"

"What?"

"You said, 'we rent the space out'. Who is 'we'?"

"Good night, Corelli."

Jules walked by him wordlessly, extinguished the only light in the room, and disappeared down the hallway. Shadows danced by the light of the moon, playfully crossing his path. The rich, dark, hues that inhabited the walls made the room feel like it was closing in on itself. Corelli felt a sense of belonging in the space – if it were possible for a wayward priest to belong. He felt as if he was being assimilated into the chamber, forever ensconced between brick and mortar.

As he turned to leave, seeking refuge through his dreams, an Alabaster statue that was nestled within a hidden nook, winked mischievously after him.

"'Wicked' is of a strange vernacular. The kids these days mean it to describe something 'cool'. Satan must be amused as he sits in the fiery depths of hell."

-Cris Corelli's Diary

Two

He awoke with dry mouth; his tongue parched from lack of booze. Trembling fingers held a cigarette as he rested in bed staring at the ceiling that was dotted with brown spots of moisture or mould. His room resembled a tent. Its sloped ceiling gave him little room to stand. He shifted and scratched at the middle of his back where it met the floor as he slept, likening the bed to a cot. An antique dresser lacked a mirror. Setting his feet upon the cold floor, he unpacked his bag and placed his mother's picture on the furniture. He used the glass in the frame to see his reflection, and as his eyes met hers, her sickly pallor forced him to look away.

They called her a "handsome woman" in her day. She was a stage actress for the local theatre, channeling many of Shakespeare's heroines. Night after night, her name occupied first place on the playbill. Her dressing room rivaled a flower shop; gifts sent by admirers both secret, and overt. Red roses were her favourite, *"The colour of passion,"* she had said in a voice mimicking Greta Garbo. Her dusty white complexion was synthetic, until the day it wasn't.

Naked, Corelli approached the only window in the room and watched as God painted the sky in shades of pink, blue, and purple. A century-old tree was adorned in Autumn foliage. He envisioned himself as a boy raking leaves next

[14]

to his father. There was always an old tune on the man's lips, thus gifting Cris his love of music.

The smoke from his cigarette stung his eyes. He snuffed it in a plastic ashtray that rested on a tiny table next to the bed, pulled on his jeans, and left his room to find the shared bathroom. Closing the door behind him, he christened himself by splashing freezing cold water on his face, and torso. The lines around his mouth and eyes were severe, put there by a decade of confessions that evoked surprise and consternation. When he smiled, those same lines were raised skyward. An attractive trait, if not an unwitting one.

Standing at the toilet, he studied the claw foot tub, pedestal sink, and the artwork on the wall that depicted a skeletal child strumming a guitar. His father had been a musician, stealing chords from other artists, until one night in the Summer of '63, a knife blade met his side in retribution. His mother had heard the news before a sold-out performance, and Juliet would never again sound as soulful.

Three resounding knocks forced him to open the door. He was greeted by a young man with long, blond hair, and piercing blue eyes.

"Sorry, man. You done in there?"

Mute, Corelli left the tiny space, retreated to his room, and dressed himself in the same red flannel shirt he

[15]

wore the previous day. Opening his Bible, he stuffed the rest of his cash between its pages, and despite their severed relationship, he willed the paltry sum to grow between God's hands.

He locked his door before descending the stairs in search of the first meal he would eat since leaving his rectory. He often thought about his congregation, who, come Sunday, would be lectured by a different man of the cloth. The Shepard who loses his sheep must continue to tend to his flock, only, he was the sheep in God's eyes.

In the meal hall, a man whose face read like an old scripture, lined with years of wisdom, looked up from his breakfast in greeting. His white hair reached his shoulders, and despite his brittle bones, he sat straight as an arrow.

"Bacon's the best in town. Name's Ol' Mike."

"Cris."

"Welcome to paradise, Cris. Kitchen's that way," Ol' Mike said, pointing with a yellowed finger.

"No table service?"

The old man laughed heartily, "Don't let Jules hear you ask that. Got the disposition of a buckin' bronco, that one does."

"Thanks for the warning," Corelli told him as he made his way to the back of the room. The windows were covered with beige shutters, stained that way by smoke, just as Ol' Mike's fingers were stained. A giant hearth occupied the far wall; extinguished, until Winter's fury urged the boarders to beg for warmth.

There was a shift in temperature as he walked, and his starved body felt the cold substantially more than that of a healthy man. It was a symptom of his disease. As alcohol and food don't mix, his weight had plummeted from a healthy 175 lbs to one-fifty. Vanity served no purpose within the priesthood, but sans collar, he felt like a plastic version of himself.

"Morning," Corelli said from the threshold of the room. He jammed his hands in his jeans' pockets to hide the fact that they were shaking.

Jules looked over her shoulder from where she stood at an industrial sized gas stove, "Morning." She walked to the island before her and leaned on it in an effort to detach herself from the man and instead, link herself with the steel. "What'll it be?"

In the bright of day, and with her hair tied away from her face, Jules' features were prominent. She was a classic beauty with big, brown eyes, high cheekbones, and a plush mouth. *Just like a horse*, Corelli thought to himself. He walked towards her, careful not to wake the sleeping giant.

"Eggs over-easy. Bacon. Toast."

"Coffee?"

"Black, please."

"Help yourself," she said, pointing with her spatula towards a large metal table housing coffee cups, cream, and sugar. "I'll just be a minute with your food."

"Thanks."

She stared at his back, curious about the man who looked like he should be on a tour bus on his way to sing to adoring fans, rather than taking up residence in a Boarding House in the middle of nowhere. She thought about the last man who had sought comfort beneath her roof, and how when he left, he took her bleeding heart with him, nourishing the earth with its purity.

She fried two eggs, added pre-cooked bacon to the plate, and two slices of toast that were already in the toaster to serve as her own breakfast. Adopting a stoic expression, she pushed Corelli's food towards him as he waited.

"There's ketchup on the tables outside."

Corelli picked up his plate and held his coffee in his other hand, "Looks great. Ol' Mike was right."

"About what?"

"The bacon. Looks good. You been working here long?" he asked, showcasing a few smile lines.

Red coloured her cheeks; put there by either embarrassment or anger. "Listen," she said, banging her spatula on her worksurface, "let's get this out of the way right now. This a business agreement. Understand? I'm not here to be your friend. Not even here for small talk. If you wanted that, you should've have made a left at the Holiday Inn. Am I making myself clear?"

At her tone, a jolt of remembrance flashed through him, reminding him of his quest to rid himself of all earthly pleasures, the first of which being that of the flesh.

"Perfectly," he told her through clenched teeth.

As Corelli was leaving, the young blond man with the blue eyes, was making his entrance, "Any coffee left?"

"Should be," Jules told him.

"Wicked."

"You got that right, kid," Corelli mumbled as he made his escape.

Like every other man who tried to make nice with the woman, he'd been thrown from the horse.

∿

He gawked at his breakfast as it swirled around the porcelain before vanishing. Beads of sweat covered his brow. His extremities adopted a purplish hue and he sat on his hands as he graced the bathroom floor, spent from forcefully eliminating the food from his shattered body. With his bile, he saw the last elements of normal life disappear. He saw, instead, a life tethered by his own sins. He was in debt with a Deity he quit believing in, and with that truth, he was no longer penitent and wanted only to drown in booze.

[19]

Standing, Corelli felt a profound feeling of hollowness, brought forth not by an empty belly, but by an empty heart. He made his way back to his room, darkened by storm clouds. Sprawling across the bed, he heard echoes of mourners as they sat and listened to a eulogy about a man who lived life recklessly. As a teenager, his sorrow enveloped him. Yet, even as he cried, his mind wandered, thinking about cars, and girls, when he should have been praying to God to take his father Home. It was a defining moment and the catalyst that would eventually lead him into a life of piety. He cursed that day, now. He swore audibly as he remembered the look of disgust on his mother's face when she realized her son's betrayal. She had led him to confession after the funeral to admit his sins to a stranger.

"Do you realize the gravity of your sin, son?"
"Yes, Father."
"Are you remorseful?"
"Yes, Father."
"Do you realize that you will burn in hell; your flesh consumed by a demon with talons for teeth, and that your violent screams will sound eternally?"

Corelli woke, disoriented. He sat up, forcing his thoughts to dissipate. It was a trick his uncle had taught him when he was young and plagued by nightmares.

"Think of a blank page. There is nothing. Not good, nor bad."

He teetered precariously on his legs, walked to the dresser, and opened the first drawer where he stored a few toiletries. Picking up a brown bottle, he unscrewed the cap, tossed two yellow pills into his mouth, and spoke to a long dead relative, "Like a *Goddamn* blank page, Uncle Joe. Like a Goddamn blank page."

"In town today, I met a woman who reminded me of my mother. She used a white cane. Although my mother had use of her eyes, she could not see me, making both women equal in their plight."

-Cris Corelli's Diary

Three

"What's your poison?"

Cris counted the liquor that lined the shelves, nearly frothing at the mouth. *The Mousetrap* was just like any other bar erected to house the drunks, and derelicts, and prey unashamedly on their vulnerabilities. The décor married frayed green carpeting, and wood paneled walls. Secrets spilled by inebriated mouths were encased within them, and he imagined the building engulfed in flames; the voices freed - drifting into unsuspecting ears.

"Well, buddy?"

The oaf who tended the bar looked as if he had stepped out of an old movie. His hair was black as tar and oiled into place. He wore a black apron, and his white shirtsleeves were rolled to his elbows to show-off his mermaid, and anchor tattoos, and one obscene tattoo depicting a nude named "Betty". To any other man, the scene would have been laughable.

"A Coke."

"Coke and what?"

"Just a Coke."

The barkeep begrudged his lost tips. "Suit yourself," he said, reserving friendly banter for his drinking customers.

Alone with his thoughts, Corelli pictured the Boarding House without a name. An unembellished piece

[23]

of wood next to the front door was almost unwelcoming in nature: "Boarding House". He was curious about the Great Room windows dressed in two-by-fours, a feature he failed to notice when he arrived; the rain and wind had helped to camouflage the exterior. He thought about his host, puzzled by her lack of zeal. Her apathy contradicted her role, and she reminded him of a death row inmate who was waiting to perish. Time and circumstance mean nothing to the man who has lost his future.

A commotion at the front door caused Corelli to vacate his seat. He attended to an older woman using a white cane. She had caught her skirts on a patron's bicycle, causing it to crash to the floor.

"Let me help," Corelli said, taking her by the elbow.

Her cheerful disposition was apparent in her greeting, "Much obliged, son. Get me to the bar now, would you? It's teatime," she said, smiling broadly.

He guided her into the seat next to his own. The bartender had delivered a bottle of Coke and a frosty glass. He emerged from the storage room and fawned over his regular.

"There, she is. The usual, Mabel?"

"You betcha."

"Comin' right up."

The woman shifted in her chair to address Corelli. Her grey hair was elegantly styled, but her cheeks were painted with too much rouge. She resembled a China Doll that had somehow aged. "Now, then. Tell me your name so that I can thank you properly."

"Cris," he said, noticing her milky irises.

"Not many folk in this town care about a blind woman. Most just look the other way. I'm indebted, Cris."

"It's no trouble." He poured the soda into the glass. The fizz was audible.

"You're new around here, aren't you?"

"Yes, ma'am. Just passing through."

"Call me Mabel. I'm not that old. Just blind."

The bartender returned with a stemmed glass holding hot tea, lemon juice, apple cider vinegar, and whiskey. He garnished the libation with a cinnamon stick. It was too fancy a drink for *The Mousetrap*, and was lovingly nicknamed, "The Mabel".

"Here you go," the barkeep said, gently touching Mabel's hand.

"Ah, teatime. Thank you, Jonah. How about a drink for my new friend here?"

"He's already got one. Coca-Cola. We got ourselves a teetotaler."

"Be nice, Jonah."

"Yeah, yeah. I'll be stocking the beer fridge. Holler if you need me."

A man older than Mabel stumbled towards the bar, drink in tow, and took a seat on Corelli's left. He was slurring the words to "Burning Down the House", and the sound of his voice grated on Corelli's already frazzled nerves.

"Mmm, delicious," Mabel said, sipping her Hot Toddy. "Where you headed, Cris?"

Corelli eyed her drink and imagined snatching it from the woman's grasp. "Anywhere is better than nowhere, I guess," he said, swallowing at the pain in his throat. He lit a cigarette to tame his shaking hands.

"You know, when my Robert was alive, we used to take long drives and deliberately get lost. I'd pack us a little wicker basket of food, and a thermos full of Robert's favourite…this very drink I'm having now. There weren't any real restrictions back then. Not like I'd let him get drunk while driving, mind you. Things were just…different." She paused and sipped from her drink to honour her love. "Anyway, my point is, it doesn't really matter where you end up. As long as you enjoyed the ride getting there. Are you married, Cris?"

The question evoked feelings of regret. The last woman he touched hadn't even revealed her name before ravishing his body with red-stained lips.

"No. My vocation wouldn't allow it."

"What vocation wouldn't allow…? Oh. I see. You're an ex-priest?"

[26]

"Yes."

"Is that why you don't drink?" she asked, innocently.

Cris smirked, "I'm an alcoholic. The priesthood had nothing to do with it."

"Isn't it hard? Being in a place like this, I mean."

His insides screamed profanities at him. The urge to drink was like a cancer, growing larger with each passing second, "Penance, I guess you'd call it."

Mabel drained her drink to destroy the evidence and quash temptation, "Do you want to talk about it, son? I'm a real good listener. In fact, did you know your other senses are heightened when you lose one? I'm blind. Perfect candidate," she said, showing off her million-dollar smile.

"Nothing to say," he said, raking his hand through his hair. "Nothing confession can fix."

The drunkard on Corelli's left was suddenly coherent. Shamefaced, he stumbled from his stool and wedged his way in between Corelli and Mabel. His wire-rimmed glasses were speckled with an unknown substance. His breath was pungent.

"Will you be so kind as to hear my confession, Father? On account that I'm dyin'?"

Mabel played with her wedding ring and listened sympathetically as Corelli tried to diffuse the situation.

"I'm sorry to hear that," Cris told him, snuffing out his cigarette.

"Been dyin' for years. Finally caught up with me. You'll do it, then? You'll hear my confession?"

"No. I can't."

"Why not? I'm sure God remembers you. You're not just like one of us now, are you?"

The silence was punctuated by an altercation at the pool tables; two men vying for their right to shoot next.

"Sorry," Corelli said, averting his gaze. He reached into his jeans for money, eager to vacate the place.

The drunk patron's eyes went wild, before drooping again. "To hell with you, then. I'm sure they're expecting you there…you bloody *fraud!*" He spat on the bar before retreating to his stool. Scanning the room for Jonah, the man shrunk in his chair, defeated.

"Damn *boor!*" Mabel said, discerning the drunk's actions. She searched the area for Corelli's arm and encircled her bony fingers around his wrist. "Don't pay him any mind, son. He has dues to pay and is out of currency."

Cris covered the woman's cold hand with his own frigid one, creating a bond between them, "I'll be leaving now, Mabel."

She nodded wearily; like a woman well-versed in being alone, "You know where to find me, if you need anyone to talk to. Off you go, now" she said into the void. "Be well."

Dropping a two-dollar bill on the mahogany, Corelli ignored the sinner to his left who was mumbling incoherently about the "asshole who deserved it", kissed Mabel on the cheek, and stepped outside.

The afternoon sun blazed above him, and as he looked at it briefly, he wondered if he had any clout left with God. Then he laughed at himself for being an imbecile. There was no loyalty program in Heaven. Admittance required a lifetime membership, and Corelli had thrown his away.

"A man came upon three doors. The first door was marked 'Safe', the second door was marked, 'Beware', and the third door was marked, 'Danger'. He entered through the third door, thinking he could prove his worth. Once inside, splendor known only to the Garden of Eden surrounded him. 'What danger can I find here?' the man asked a beautiful woman unlike any he's ever seen. 'You fool,' she cried, enveloping him within her arms."

-Cris Corelli's Diary

Four

Corelli stood with his back against the wall, hidden behind the open door of the office. He listened to the tinny sound of laughter as it emerged from wee lungs. It was dwarfed by Jules' laughter; displaced in the bowels of the Boarding House.

"What happened next?" asked a young female.

"Well, the notebooks fill a dusty attic where no one ever visits."

"The books they wrote in when they weren't dead?"

"Yes. At night, when everyone else is sleeping downstairs, the two souls come alive and meet again, revisiting the memories they once shared."

"Wait! Stop!" the young girl said excitedly. "What does re-visit-ing mean?"

Corelli held his breath and focused on the bare wall before him to temper the sound of his beating heart. *Blank paper. Blank paper. Blank paper.*

"It's like when you talk about old times."

"Oh."

"When the sun wakes, they climb back between the pages, where love is eternal."

"Eternal?"

"Forever and ever," Jules explained. "So, did you like the story?"

The little girl was quiet, and then shouted, "Oh, yes, I did! I want to find a book like that one day."

"So that you can live with someone forever?"

"Well, not really. I kinda like being alone. Maybe you can come live with me, though."

Jules kissed the child on the top of her head, and hugged her to her heart, "I think we should get you home, now."

"Can I come back tomorrow?"

"Maybe. We'll check with your dad, okay?"

Cris saw her through the cracks between the door hinges, rising from the threadbare orange couch, and retrieving a tiny coat from the chair across from her desk. He slipped away unnoticed and ascended the stairs, stomping deliberately to make his presence known. His heart plunged further into his stomach with each step. His surreptitious desires held him captive. Escaping from himself proved futile, and like every other time in his life when he played with the devil, he felt its greasy claws hook in his back, dragging him Underworld.

Safe behind his locked door and guided by his own insatiable hunger, he shed his clothes and met the floor where he felt more at home.

He felt closer to Satan.

~

"That's it? Fuck sakes," she cursed, pulling down her pink Lycra minidress.

"I'm sorry. Sometimes, when I drink…"

"Save it. Where's my money?"

"You didn't say anything about money."

"I don't fucking believe this. You thought I was just hot for you? Thanks, for nothing, sailor."

The harlot banged the stall door shut, leaving him alone, and unfulfilled. Bang, bang, bang…

Jules knocked harder, "Corelli? You in there? You missed two meals today. Like I said, no refunds."

He opened the door, stared briefly at the tray she was holding, and resumed his position on the bed with his head in his hands. He sought asylum from himself. He was sick of being alone, bound to the bed with invisible shackles.

Jules crossed the threshold and quietly closed the door behind her. She placed his dinner on the dresser and leaned against the wall, her arms crossed over her fragile heart.

"Brought you food. Don't get used to it, though."

The silence was almost tangible. The sun had set, and she brought a lamp to life to facedown his demons. Rubbing her hands up and down her jeans, she inched closer to where he was sitting.

"Is it a headache? I have Aspirin."

[33]

The unmistakeable sound of weeping filled the room, canceling the notion that boys don't cry. What little was left of her heart, bled for him. Kneeling at his feet, she adopted a motherly look, and began the process of dismantling the wall between them.

"Hey. Talk to me."

Corelli lifted his head and stared right through her. His eyes were telling. Within them, she saw stories untold; clandestine snippets of a barren life.

"I'm thirsty, Jules," he said, tilting an imaginary bottle towards his lips.

Understanding registered in her eyes. She came to her feet and stood back against the wall, seeking support. "Lost a brother that way. Did you come here to detox?"

His sighs were endless. "No."

Wordlessly, she walked to the dresser and retrieved a plate that held a thick pork chop, mashed potatoes, and boiled vegetables. She set it on the table next to the bed and handed him cutlery that was rolled into a paper napkin.

"Eat."

Too weary to argue, he pierced one green bean and ate it without pleasure. Satisfied, Jules roamed around the small room, stopping in front of the dresser. "Your mom?"

"Yes."

"She's beautiful."

"Was."

"What?" she asked him, twisting her head in his direction.

"Was. Past tense. She's dead."

She looked away. "I'm sorry," she told his mother's likeness.

It was quiet, save for the sound of his knife and fork scraping against the dish. Jules walked to the windowsill and ran her fingers across his Bible. The leather was peeling along the spine, but the gilded pages shined in the near darkness of the room.

"Above all, love each other deeply, because love covers over a multitude of sins."

"Peter 4:8."

"You know it?" Jules asked, facing him.

"I know all of it."

"You don't strike me as the Church-going type, Corelli."

He saw the Roman Collar before his eyes, muddied, and soiled by his own admissions. His gaze drifted to Jules' svelte form. She was fresh-faced, and without makeup, she seemed timid, and unlike the stony-hearted woman he had first met. They were both stripped of their costumes.

"How's the pork?"

"Dry as hell."

Her laugh was therapeutic. She shook her head causing her ponytail to swing back and forth. "Serves me right for trying to do a guy a favour…"

Corelli stood as she approached his door to leave. His countenance gave him away as a drowning man. "Can I ask you something, Jules?"

"What?" she asked, her hand on the doorknob.

"Who is 'we'?"

Her face lost colour. Letting go of the knob, she stood with her back against the wood, her palms flat against it, as if hoping to be swallowed by it. She spoke quickly and without a pause in her speech, wishing to rid herself of the words.

"I think you know there's no 'we', Corelli. He took off. Just left in the middle of the night. Was here just like you are. Said he wanted a room. Then he said he wanted me." She crossed her hands behind her back, to ward off Cupid's wrath. "I should have listened to my mama when she told me that love is make-believe. I thought she was crazy. I saw how daddy looked at her…how much he loved her. When the war took him away, it was like I made him up. It was like he never existed. 'We' is fake. It will always be fake. There's no 'we'. Not for me, anyway. I only tell people that so that they stay the *fuck* away from me."

His utterances went unspoken. She struggled to open the door and slammed it shut, trapping him inside, alone, with nothing but his wretched thoughts.

Five Years Earlier

"Bless me, Father, for I have sinned. It's been two weeks since my last confession. No, wait...it's been three weeks since my last confession."

Hidden in shadows, Father Corelli grinned. He shifted uncomfortably in the confessional that steamed in the late July heat. He recognized the man kneeling next to him as Irwin Trade, a stout, awkward man who, despite his thirty-one years, lived with his mother. There was a lag in his confession, and when he spoke, it was with a noticeable quaver.

"I have to admit that I'm scared, Father."

"Blessed is the man whose sin the Lord does not count against him and in whose spirit is no deceit."

"Amen, Father. Amen."

"What's troubling you?"

Irwin chose his words fastidiously; each word laced with an essence of a camp side ghost story. "Well, you see, Father...it's like this. It always takes a good four inches of hot oil to fry the onion rings. Too little oil, and they don't crisp up, you know? About a week ago, we were talking and cooking, just like always when the joint closes for the night. Ma turned the lock on the door, balanced the till and then joined me in the kitchen. Business isn't very good, Father. It's bad, actually. Real bad, and I can't sleep at night."

[38]

The sun filtered through the stained-glass windows, brilliantly colouring Madonna, and Son. Father Corelli counted the beads on his rosary; *34, 36, 37*. He felt the sweat drip down his back like a rivulet. The heat was stifling, and his mind drifted to other things.

"…bitching and screaming as if it's all my fault. You know? Can I say 'bitching', Father?"

"Go on," the Father said, clearing the cobwebs from his throat.

"So anyway, I lost my temper. I…it sure is hot in here, ain't it, Father? So, like I was saying, I lost my temper. I couldn't take the sound of her voice. It was like a screeching cat. Nag, nag, *nag!* That's all she ever did was nag. To this day, I think of swear words as terms of endearment. She sure liked to remind me what an asshole I am."

The priest adjusted his robes. Irwin's tone had become insidious, laced with ghastly undertones; something nefarious lurking in the deepest recesses of his mind.

"It was reflex. I didn't mean to. Maybe I did…I don't know, but after it was over, I couldn't take my eyes off her. It wasn't the screams that got to me. It was how I could see her skin melting off."

Paralyzed with an all-consuming fear, the Father succumbed to Lucifer, and purged all things sacred. *Blank paper. Blank paper. Blank paper.* The walls closed in on him, sending him closer to a lunatic.

"Did you hear me, Father?" Irwin asked, knocking softly on the wall between them. The air was polluted with things unsaid. A mouse scampered outside the confessional, seeking refuge. "When she passed out, I had to hoist her up using the dessert trolley. Took a long time, but I couldn't tell the cops it was an accident. How do you get that much oil on your face by accident? It took three days for the body to burn, but after that, I was able to open for business. Pizza oven's working again. That's good, at least."

I once delivered a sermon about a man who

dreamed of winning the lottery and played

two dollars a week for fifty years.

He never won a dime. Had he saved his

money he'd be $5200 richer.

A small sum compared to the hope he felt.

One parishioner scoffed, "I'd rather have the

money, Father."

I told him, "There's no currency in Heaven."

-Cris Corelli's Diary, October 12th, 1985

Five

God was shining through the trees. Their branches waved in greeting. Corelli sat on the front steps of the Boarding House smoking cigarettes in succession. He was lost in thought, reminiscing about his childhood and the dead dreams he left behind. As a kid, he loved to tumble and taught himself how to do backflips. Italy had dominated boxing at the 1960 Summer Olympics, and to honour his heritage, he had wanted to follow in the footsteps of those athletes. Then, selfishly, his father died. The casket had been surrendered to the earth, unrepentant.

In Seminary, he had immoral thoughts, negating celibacy in his mind. He was infatuated with Samantha Worthington, a shy, dark-haired girl who occupied the office. She always wore a pink headband in her hair and carried a pink purse. Her smile warmed him, but it was everything she didn't say that made him lust after her; imagining the fantasies that whirled around her lovely head. Late at night, Samantha would visit him in his dreams, whispering things profane, satisfying his carnal desires. He would see her the next day, sitting posh and pretty, oblivious to his obsession. On a warm Spring morning, she had arrived at work sporting a diamond on her finger, and she became ordinary in his mind.

Corelli flicked his smoke in front of him and lit a new one. Leaving his place on the steps, he strolled the perimeter of the building. He had spent the previous day holed up in his room, reading, and doing everything possible to avoid seeing Jules. She had shown him her festering wounds, and although he was trained to absorb other people's pain, he had no words of guidance to offer someone whose broken heart beat in tandem with his own.

On the south side of the building, Cris paused to rest his hand against the brick, in part to feel the warmth of the sun penetrating his palm, but mostly, it was a habit he has employed since he was young -- to be able to feel the essence confined within a structure. Staring straight up, he saw her silhouette fill a second story window, and he quickly looked away lest she see him.

"'Bout a hundred years."

Corelli spun around to greet Ol' Mike who was holding a rake in his hands, more for show, than anything else, "What?"

"This building. Circa 1882."

Cris flipped the collar of his leather jacket to break the wind that had suddenly picked up speed. He studied the man's face, trying to see past the whiskers and lines, and catch a glimpse of who Young Mike might have been. "You been here long?"

"About as long as Jules. Three months, give or take."

"This place has only been open three months?"

Ol' Mike raked a few leaves, building a little pile at his feet. "No. Someone else ran it before her. She answered a caretaker ad in the newspaper. Guess she got more than she bargained for."

"What do you mean?"

"Quit twenty years ago, but I could use one of those," he said, jutting his chin towards the smoke drifting around them.

Corelli pulled his cigarettes from his inside pocket and offered one to the old man. He brought a match to life, shielded it between his hands, and lit Mike's smoke.

"Thanks."

"What about Jules?"

"You've got eyes, son. Too young and beautiful to be stuck here."

"She's not in prison. She can leave."

Grey clouds shaded the sun while Ol' Mike ruminated. Corelli swore that he could hear his father's song beneath the wind, but his voice was silenced by the old man's melancholic refrain.

"Stuck here by her own blood." He dropped his rake and walked towards a green striped vinyl lawn chair. Its aluminum was rusted, and it bent precariously with Mike's weight. "You ever feel the world shake? Not by Mother Nature's hand, mind you."

"Felt the whole Goddamned earthquake," Cris told him.

The man nodded wearily. "I never knew what death sounded like. Most times I witnessed it, it was quiet. Came in, took what it wanted, and left. That night, her screams echoed throughout the place. Every crevice was filled with her wails. Still hear it sometimes...when night grows unfriendly," he said, dropping his smoke in front of him. He crushed it with one well-worn boot; its sole was thin, and riddled with holes, personifying an arduous life.

"What happened?" Cris asked, walking towards him.

"Lost her baby," the old man said, curbing his emotions. "Happened a month ago. I suppose she feels like she can't leave...that somehow, that child is still here."

Instinctively, Corelli raised his head towards the second story window which, despite being void of any human form, he saw a spectral figure rocking a swaddled infant. He faced Mike who was examining his fingernails to dissuade further questions.

"There was a man in the picture. When did he leave?"

"Right before she miscarried," Mike said in unison with a crow's caw. "Gotta get back to work," he said, wobbling on his thin legs. He accepted the rake from Corelli and began mindlessly piling leaves at his feet. Raising his eyes above his fringe, he watched as Corelli walked away and disappeared around the corner of the house. Whispering, he addressed the spirits that surrounded him, *"Let me be. He was bound to figure it out on his own."*

∼

Hostile voices washed over him as he stood in full view in the office doorway. His fingers inched towards his neck where his noose once was. The liberty to think for himself had been stolen by a divine warden: prisoner of thoughts. Peeling himself of the collar had allowed him to regain his voice. It was both a blessing, and a curse.

"Give me a minute, Corelli."

He nodded and stepped just out of their line of vision, ready to pounce on the guy who was blatantly disrespecting the Lady of the Manor.

"She enjoys it," Jules was saying. "You didn't mind before now."

"Well, now I mind!" the nameless man said, pounding a fist on the oak desk. "Tell her today. I'll bring her by in an hour. She has better things to do than fill her head with fairy tales by the likes of you."

"The likes of me?"

"White trash."

The man sped past Corelli wordlessly. His gait was lopsided, causing him to smash into a wall before making his exit, reminding Cris of the countless nights he spent sparring with the devil while skunk-drunk.

"You coming in, or what?"

Corelli charged in, ready to lambast the guy, but stopped short at the look on Jules' face. She was sullen, trying to hide her feelings by reorganizing an already organized desk.

"Who was that?"

She froze, a stapler in her hand to serve as a weapon if she needed it, "That's what you wanted?"

"No."

"What do you want, then? I don't have all day."

His eyes briefly drifted towards her empty belly, "It's not important."

"Good," she said, resuming her actions.

"Jules."

"What!?"

The imaginary noose tightened around his throat, "Fuck it." Corelli turned to leave, aware that her eyes were searing a hole through his back.

"Wait, *Goddamnit*...her name is Ella," Jules said, stumbling backwards into her chair. She buried her face in her hands. Her words were forced, as if she were being interrogated. Corelli found his place on the orange sofa and lit a cigarette. The thin stream of smoke was like a line between them; one he dared not cross.

"I heard you the other day. Telling stories."

Jules dropped her hands but didn't admonish him. She rose from her chair and paced the floor between them, before stopping and sitting on the edge of her desk. "I told him that she enjoys it. The truth is, I enjoy it. I kinda love the kid, if you want to know the truth. I'm such an *idiot!*" she said, rocking back and forth like a mental patient.

Corelli leaned forward to better listen. It was a practice he had exercised during his vocation as a harbinger of hope.

"Was that her father?"

Jules nodded.

"Why doesn't he want her to come here anymore?"

"Jesus Christ, you sure ask a lot of questions for someone who hides."

"What the fuck does that mean?"

"Nothing," she said, standing. Her sleeve met her face to dry her tears. She tamed a few strands of hair back in place and toyed with her belt buckle. "He'll be back soon. If you don't mind, Corelli…"

"You want me to leave?"

Jules sifted through a pile of books, searching for Ella's favourite. "Yeah," she said, without looking up.

"I can stay. To…"

[48]

"To what?" she asked, meeting his eyes. "Protect me? Beat the guy up? Don't make me laugh."

"Don't flatter yourself," he said, submitting to his Italian temper.

"Then get the fuck out. *Christ!*"

Tossing his half-finished smoke in a crystal ashtray, he took four long strides towards her desk. A gold crucifix spilled from her neckline as she leaned over a stack of poetry books. He recoiled, as if being singed by the Talisman.

"Nice necklace."

She stood tall and tucked the cross back into her sweater, "Making fun of me, now?"

The harsh baby blue colour on her lids did not betray her beauty. Her eyes were dull, though, like the veneer of his mother's dining room table where he sat alone most nights. They stared each other down, denying what resided in their fractured hearts.

"They were right," he told her, grinning.

"Who was right?"

"'Hell hath no fury like a woman scorned'. I'll be upstairs if you need me."

Her rebuttal died on her tongue. Alone, she retrieved the symbol of her religion and kissed it. In his room, time and space aligned as his fingers met his lips.

"Pink roses bloom outside the boarding house. I imagine their roots entangled like the legs of spent lovers."

-Cris Corelli's Diary, October 13th, 1985

Six

Corelli woke before dawn. His dreams had been riddled with ghastly images of infection and disease. His pus-filled sores covered his entire body. Seconds before opening his eyes, he was standing at the pulpit, facing a congregation made up of alien-like creatures with indescribable deformities.

Masked beneath the stream of water from the showerhead, he shed tears of contrition. In his youth, he was brought up to believe that Hell was not fire and brimstone, but a place where one's past sins would forever haunt the offender. He was now a prisoner to those thoughts, and unashamedly, he was afraid.

Back in his room, he dressed quickly, feeling a deep chill in his bones. He picked up his Bible and immediately set it back in its place, as the words no longer consoled him, but seemed to mock him for his transgressions. Swallowing two more yellow pills, he crept down the stairs and closed the front door behind him. In the darkness, he felt invisible to the world, and he welcomed the tranquility that enveloped him -- however fleeting.

With a smoke between his lips, he picked three untarnished roses that grew wild along the front of the house. He watched as the blood trickled down his finger.

The thorns were like a metaphor for his life, serrated and jagged; never unencumbered.

Inside the house, he walked towards the kitchen in search of a receptacle for the flowers. Opening a bottom cupboard, he crouched down, and blindly felt his way until he touched something recognizable. He caressed an empty wine bottle like a lover caresses the curves of his lady; his desire, the same.

Carrying the flowers to her office, he set the makeshift vase on the corner of her desk, and as the sun rose, he deemed it intrusive; his nightly sojourn, postponed.

∾

"Bacon and eggs?"

"Please."

Jules plated his food robotically. She had let her hair loose, and it cascaded over half her face, repelling niceties, and rehearsed greetings from her boarders.

In the meal hall, Corelli ate a hurried breakfast, making small talk with Kurt who rambled on about his adventures in surfing and his desire to capture the perfect wave. His long, blond hair was tucked behind his ears, and despite the cooler weather, he wore a sleeveless t-shirt featuring an *MTV* logo, and cut-off jean shorts. Corelli masticated at the soiled memories of his youth and felt an unreasonable animosity towards the young man whose only crime was to exist. He left him sitting alone and carried his half-eaten meal to the kitchen where Jules stood at the sink wrapping her dark locks around each other to form a bun.

"I'm going into town, if you need anything."

Startled, she turned abruptly towards the doorway and quickly let her hair down, but it was a vain attempt to hide. A red bruise encircled her puffy eye, exposing Corelli to the truth. He tossed his plate on the steel counter, causing it to break in half, like the pieces of his heart.

"Where is he?"

"Corelli…"

"Where the *fuck* is he, Jules?"

"It won't do any good! Just leave it, okay?" she said, tying her hair back up. She turned her back on him and scrubbed furiously at a pan. "And clean up your mess…please."

Ignoring her, Corelli stormed out of the kitchen. He ran up the stairs towards his room and met Ol' Mike on the second-floor landing.

"Mike, listen. Do you know the little girl who comes here? To visit with Jules?"

There was dread in the old man's eyes that matched the fury in Corelli's. His words were laced with trepidation, "I know her."

"Where does she live?"

Ol' Mike looked left, and then right, as if conferring with the mythical creature on each shoulder.

"Tell me!" Cris pleaded through clenched teeth.

"About a mile east from here on the main road. There's an old, rusted tractor on the front lawn." He grasped Corelli's forearm in warning, "I don't know what you're thinking, but I wouldn't do anything foolish, son."

A stream of sunlight shone through a crack in the boarded-up window beside them, causing dust to hover like finely spun gossamer. Corelli freed himself from the man's grasp. Syllables latched together with finality, "I would," he said, taking the rest of the stairs two at a time.

Behind closed doors, Corelli made the sign of the cross, calling upon an old Friend.

"Wise men lead battles. Fools win them."

-Cris Corelli's Diary

Seven

Plumes of smoke were visible in the distance, emanating from the smokestacks from the factory in town where blue collar workers spent their days transforming pulp into paper. At the turn of the 20th Century, a paper merchant from New York settled his family in Canada, and valiantly forged ahead, despite the braces he wore on his legs resulting from a childhood bout with Polio. When founder, Jeffrey Robinson-Wright died in 1956, his ghost took up residence in the heart of the factory, shouting orders from silenced lips.

Corelli's long legs propelled him forward. His eyes darted across the roadway, searching for the rusted tractor that adorned a barbarian's lawn. Despite his aversion to conflict, he clenched his fists at regular intervals, like the Olympians he wished to mimic before his dreams dissolved into oblivion.

Paved road gave way to gravel, and then to dirt. He thought of her. He thought of her as something mythical, like the goddesses on religious plaquettes that have since been relinquished into the greedy hands of museum curators. She fought with tenacity, born of torment; her guise was like granite, easily fragmented beneath the weight of a heavy heart.

Corelli paused at the sight of an archaic structure occupying an overgrown lawn. Its rusted bones were like the old Chevy that rested in the middle of the woods behind his childhood home. The neighbourhood children had christened the car graveyard, "Dead Wheel Alley", and it was there that he first succumbed to profound sexual urges with a skinny brunette sporting eyes that were too large for her face. The tryst had bordered on being vulgar, and she had thanked him with half a peanut butter and jelly sandwich she had made just for the occasion. Fifteen years later, they found her propped against a dumpster as cats foraged on her decaying body.

He made his way up a twisty dirt driveway and stood on the dilapidated porch, straining to hear voices. Bob Barker's familiar drawl reached his ears. He knocked with a closed fist and waited, imagining how the scenario would play out. As if manipulated by a poltergeist, the door swung fully open. He looked down to see Ella gazing up at him with chocolate smeared across her chubby cheeks.

"Daddy says we don't want any."

Crouching at eye level with the girl, Corelli said, "You must be Ella."

Tiny hands met tiny hips, "How do you know my name?"

"I'm a friend of Jules," he told her, smiling.

Excited, Ella ran past him, and down the steps. "Is she *here!?"*

"Well, no, but…"

"Ella! Get back in the house. *Now!"*

Corelli turned towards the doorway where a man wearing only boxers and a sleeveless t-shirt stood with a can of beer in one hand. His girth matched his height, and fire reflected from his eyes, the same way it did when he sped past Corelli in the boarding house. Cris waited while Ella huffed and puffed her way up the stairs. Her father's hand met her shoulder.

"Go clean up. Then clean up the kitchen. You hear me?"

"Yes," the girl squeaked out nervously.

"What!?"

"Yes, daddy."

The man pushed her inside and closed the door. He joined Corelli on the porch that sunk, slightly, with too much pressure.

"State your peace, and then leave."

Corelli met his gaze, confident in his mission to beat the man to a pulp. He leaned backwards to see a spectator peeking through the sheer, moth-eaten curtains that lined the living room window, and used his words as daggers instead.

"My name is Cris."

"Did I ask what your name is? What do you want?" the man asked, chugging from his beer.

Corelli clenched his jaw until his teeth hurt and quietly recited a prayer that went unheard. He was reminded of his nightmares where discarded relics evidenced the lives of fallen Sisters and Brothers, condemned to a fiery hereafter for betraying God's spoken word.

"Fuck sakes, speak!"

Jolted back to the present, he addressed the savage in layman's terms. "There's a special place in hell for men who beat on women. I suggest you get on your knees if you want to give up your seat. Right after you apologize to Jules."

The brute chewed obnoxiously on his lower lip. He downed the rest of his drink and tossed the crumpled can to the side, into a bush. Wiping his hand across his dirty mouth, he admitted the extent of his callousness, "Would sooner burn."

Corelli smirked, imagining the man's blubber melting like a wax dummy in a crematorium. The door opened. Ella emerged with cheeks red from scrubbing too hard. She hung onto her father's arm, acting scared, as if she's played the part before. The man grinned victoriously, and in a fake fatherly voice, told her, "It's okay, pumpkin. I'll only be another minute. Go on back in the house."

Privy to their ploy, Corelli played the card he had been hiding up his sleeve, "Yes, go back in and get your jacket and shoes. Jules is excited to see you."

The child's eyes grew wide as circles, "Really?" she asked, tugging on her dad's arm, "I can go see Jules, daddy?"

The proverbial steam escaped from the man's ears. "Yeah," he said, cold as ice. "Go on, now."

"Yay! Be right back, mister!"

Alone, the men glared at one another. The Neanderthal spoke first, slightly slurring his words, "You think you're smart, eh?"

"Just trying to make two ladies happy."

"Get the fuck off my porch, scumbag."

"Glad to," he said, turning. Twisting back around, Corelli bid the man good-bye with a final warning. "If I ever see so much of a scratch on Jules again, *God help me,* I'll kill you with my own bare hands."

He walked down the steps and stood waiting for Ella who ran out the door with a stuffed bunny in tow. She waved at her father who spat profanities at Corelli before retreating into his house and slamming his door shut.

Walking hand-in-hand, the unlikely pair strolled back towards the boarding house, oblivious to the despicable activity that was taking place inside the tumbledown house they left behind.

~

"I don't go to school. Daddy says teachers are stupid. Even Sister Mary Margaret at Sunday School."

They held Floppy between them. The stuffed rabbit swung lazily and in tandem with Corelli's brief, choppy steps so as not to fatigue Ella whose short legs worked overtime.

A murder of crows lined the top of a fence. Corelli remembered the tales his late aunt used to tell. The flock was supposed to portend a death. He had always dismissed the woman's ramblings as folklore. She had died a spinster and a plain marker was erected to commemorate a life barely lived, having died by her own hand on the cusp of her thirtieth birthday.

"Did you like Sunday School?"

"We had cookies."

Corelli looked down at his new friend and smiled, "Cookies are good."

"Yeah, but they wouldn't let us eat them until we learned how to stop tempting."

"You mean, 'temptation'?"

She bobbed her head up and down. "How did you know?" she asked, kicking at a stone on the path. "Did you go to Sunday School, too?"

Tired of swinging her arm, Ella hugged Floppy to her chest. She yawned, alerting Corelli to the purple bruises

[61]

beneath her eyes; the delicate skin blemished by sleeplessness.

"Are you tired? Do you want me to carry you?"

"No. Daddy says that's for babies. What Sunday School did you go to?"

"Actually," Corelli said, lighting a cigarette, "it's called a Seminary."

Ella wrinkled her nose, "What did you learn there?"

"How to be a priest."

She stopped dead in her tracks, holding Floppy by one ear, "You're a *priest?"* she asked, exaggerating the last word. "You don't look like a priest."

"I'm not one anymore."

"Oh. Like daddy," she said, walking as if along an invisible tightrope. "He used to work fixing things but stopped when I was born."

"What do you mean?"

"Mommy left when I was born."

Corelli tossed his smoke to the side, contemplating his next question, and the effect it might have on an eight-year old. "Do you...do you know where she went?"

"Oh yes I do."

"Where, Ella?"

"Heaven. Look!" she said, pointing to the boarding house as it came into view. "We're here!"

She ran a short distance ahead of him, innocence pushing her forward; her dreams caught on the wind.

"Hurry *up,* Cris!"

He jogged a few feet, catching up to her, and as her hand reached for his, he caved to her child-like fervor. Lifting her onto his shoulders, the little girl inched closer to the sky and Corelli made friends with God.

"I remember how I marvelled at God's hand in nature, when on one occasion, a peacock blue sky suddenly turned grey as gravel and the clouds spent their tears. The sands emptied and I was left with my own private sanctuary. I still feel that rain on my skin."

-Cris Corelli's Diary

Eight

A gentle rain danced upon the windowpane with no discernible pattern. Corelli wished for a wicked tempest to come and wash away the refuse that sullied the earth, whether man, or beast disguised in man's clothing. Ella's father was a beast, exempt from moral obligation. He used force on a woman. His scales were showing.

When sleep eluded him, Corelli would often lie awake and debate the origin of evil. Despite his spiritual life, he would often adhere to the notion that humans are not born with sin, but that dire circumstance can successfully make one turn to the other side where monsters dwell, spurning salvation.

Footfall alerted him. His door was slightly ajar. Jules pushed on it with one finger to find him sitting up in bed, scrawling in a notebook. She was used to spewing tepid words, but the scent of roses still lingered, softening her heart.

He looked up at her, curious. After having left Ella in Jules' welcoming arms, he had whittled the afternoon away by writing odd musings, and documenting snippets of his past. The diary was more like a log, meant to be read long after his death to memorialize his spirit, and introduce him to an incognizant world. At times, the words bled on the page, marred by his sins.

Jules leaned against the doorjamb with one hip. Her voice sounded timid, bordering on demure. "Can I come in?"

"Yes."

"Don't get too excited. Found it at a garage sale," she said, depositing a ghetto blaster at the foot of the bed. "I noticed your cassette tapes when I was changing your towels. They aren't much use without this."

Corelli ran his fingers across the music-player, sensing old tunes emanating from it.

"Thank you."

"You're welcome."

She turned to leave, having relayed her gratitude regarding Ella with a gift.

He stood and approached her, keeping a respectable space between them. "Stay. I'll play some tunes."

The skin around her eye had turned blue. His heart hurt, noticing the makeup she chose for her other eye – a matching smoky hue. Turning her back on him, she left wordlessly.

Corelli kicked the door closed. He lit a smoke, wishing to choke on his own shortcomings, and he grew disgusted by the way that affliction seems to favour the downtrodden, like the couple who are evicted from their house, only to be met with sickness.

"Are you going to help me with this thing, or what?" Jules asked, swinging his door wide. She was awkwardly balancing a chair in one hand, and two opened bottles of Coke in the other, effectively dissolving the black cloud over his head.

He went to her and took the chair from her, placing it across from his bed where she sat facing him. He accepted the Coke she was offering, strangling the bottle beneath his quivering fingers.

"Cheers," she said, raising her drink in his direction. "So, you going to play DJ?"

He placed his Coke on the nightstand and plugged the ghetto blaster into the same outlet as the floor lamp. Rummaging through his drawers, he chose the tape featuring "Bus Stop", his favourite song by *The Hollies*.

"It works."

"Thank God for that, or I'd be out five bucks."

Musical notes matched the rhythm of the rain that continued to fall from a darkened sky. The Tiffany-inspired lamp cast a romantic shadow over everything. He rejected the sentimental feelings gnawing at his insides and employed a friendly demeanor, killing the butterflies in his belly. When she spoke, the butterflies were resurrected.

"I want to thank you for what you did today. With Ella."

He shrugged. "She's a great kid."

[67]

"The feeling's mutual, it would seem. She told me all about *Father Cris.*"

Lightning struck simultaneously with the reference. God was angry.

"She told you?"

Jules took a gulp of her drink and placed the bottle at her bare feet. Her long, red, tunic matched the stain on her lips. Her black jeans hugged her lean legs. "What did you expect? Little girls *do* kiss and tell."

Extinguishing his smoke, Corelli threaded his fingers through his thick hair. He felt exposed; his soul, naked. "I left the priesthood before coming here."

"I figured. How are you holding up?"

Feeling less like a man, and more like an impostor, he avoided her question by changing the music.

"Have you always lived here?" he asked over his shoulder.

"This shithole town? No. Not even the homeless squat here. I grew up in Montreal."

"You're French."

"Can't speak a word, actually. But I used to love going to the Jean-Talon Market. The colours are what got to me. Fruit and vegetables from every hue in the spectrum. Inspired my love of cooking...and you can keep your jokes about my pork chops to yourself, Corelli."

Walking over to the nightstand, he shook a cigarette out of its package, and offered it to Jules. Inches separated them as he leaned into her to be able to light it. Her perfume wafted towards his nose – something reminiscent of apple pie.

"July, eh? How'd that happen?" he asked, sitting on the edge of the bed.

"I was born in July. My parents had zero imagination. My brother started calling me Jules, and it kinda stuck. I prefer it, anyway."

"It suits you," he told her, lighting his own smoke.

She dragged her chair closer to the ashtray, and to him. "No, it doesn't. Sounds more like it should belong to some high-class sophisticate. Someone beautiful."

"You don't know, do you?"

"Know what?" she asked him, laughing.

"Never mind."

"What, Corelli?"

"My mom was a stage actress," he said, reclining with his elbows on the mattress. "Had all kinds of admirers. She used to say that it was part of the job, and if Tom, Dick or Harry wasn't around, it meant she wasn't pretty enough and she should hit the want-ads."

"Which one are you? Tom, Dick or Harry?"

He smirked. "I have eyes," he said, echoing Ol' Mike.

[69]

Jules snuffed out her half-smoke and walked to his dresser. She picked up the photograph, studying it. "You have *her* eyes," she said. "How did she die?"

Sitting up, his tone changed. Her ghost lingered in the corner of the room, chastising him. Memories flooded his brain like locust. "Horribly," he told her. "Like everyone else."

"That bad, eh? I'm sorry," she added, truthfully.

A deafening boom shook the boarding house, causing Jules to drop his mother's picture.

"Dammit!" she said, crouching to pick it up, "I should have guessed by the lightning. I'm a little on edge. I'm sorry," she said, checking the frame for damage.

She saw his hand in her line of vision. He had joined her on the floor; an innocent act that forced her backwards, frightened.

"Hey. It's okay," he said, standing. He helped her to her feet. The moisture from her hand mingled with his. "It's understandable."

"What is?"

"That you're on edge," he said, his hand inching towards her cheek.

"*Back off,* Corelli!" she said, meeting the wall behind her.

"I was just..."

"Using this," she said, pointing to her head, "as an excuse to touch me."

"No. You're wrong."

Lyrics embodying love were lost between them. They were adults seeking a magic cure, like the wonder that illuminates a child's eyes and grows dimmer as the years pass. Answers remained in an obscure place, tainted by too many memories.

The power failed, mercifully ending their discourse. He brought a match to life, allowing her to find her way out.

The sound of the door opening was like sandpaper scraping against his heart. Turning towards him, she stared into the darkness, eyes aglow – like the huntress scavenging for love.

Three Years Earlier

"Forgive me, Father, for I have sinned. It's been many years since my last confession, and I'm sorry about that. Really, I am. So, I'd appreciate it if you wouldn't interrupt me. If maybe I can confess, and maybe you can just listen? Thank you, Father.

I have to start by telling you that my first love was a shattered hippie who wanted to change the world. He loved to defy the rules. He was a nocturnal creature, steadfast in his resolve – with a brilliant, damaged mind. I started to wonder if he fulfilled his dreams, or if he still thought of me...if he missed me.

One day, I jumped in my car, intent to leave my world behind. I went to him. I wasn't in denial. I knew where I was going, driving along the beaten path where the other lovelorn travelled to unknown destinations, with only our memories to keep me company. It was thrilling, Father. It was like an adventure. I felt like a young woman again. I felt tenderer.

When I arrived, I sat in my car a long time. I looked upon the clapboard house with a mix of nostalgia and regret...for all the things that I didn't say. Do you know what I mean, Father? I knew he still lived there. I had called Information before I left. I almost wished that he had moved somewhere far away like he always planned on doing. I definitely wish it now.

She was gorgeous. When she opened the door, my jaw literally dropped. Golden locks, and a superstar figure. I noticed the diamond right away. Huge, by today's standards and my first thought was, 'How could he afford a gem of that value?'. I was jealous, Father. So jealous that I didn't try to hide it. I demanded to know where he was. I refused to tell her my name. I wanted only to speak to him. I cursed her.

Then something happened. I felt my entire body pulsating with desire. She kept calling his name, *'Gavin! Gavin!'*. The more she screamed, the more I felt myself on the brink of ecstasy. Then I saw him. I saw him descending the staircase like some male version of Scarlett O'Hara. He had lost all of his gorgeous hair, and gained at least forty pounds, and still, my whole body shook with pleasure, and before I knew it, Father, I came right there...on their doorstep."

"Those delights we tackle in a state of reverie become our downfall. Full bellies, numbed minds, serve to define us. Zombie-like, we sit and stare through the fog. We call it a feast of thanks. The unfortunate call it 'abundance'. Sharing is our only saving grace."

-Cris Corelli's Diary,
Thanksgiving, October 14th, 1985

Nine

It was raining leaves. The sun's brilliance blinded him, and he shielded his vulnerable eyes with one arm. He had opted out of breakfast, deciding, instead, to explore the wooded area across from the boarding house where man is tricked into believing that they are alone on Earth. As a child, he saw the world through a lens. He liked to examine rocks, pebbles, leaves, his Cheerios. Mimicking a mad scientist, he carried around a magnifying glass in his back pocket. Like so many childhood mementos, it was discarded, along with his innocence.

He saw a toad in his path; distended belly and warted skin. Sidestepping the creature, he met a tree branch headfirst. Its petrified fingers nearly poked at his eye, and he thought of Mabel and her husband, youthful and gay, picnicking somewhere remote and secluded from the world. He dismissed the vision, envious of an old woman's scrapbook.

Approaching the road, he saw her on the steps of the boarding house flailing her arms. He ran to her with his heart in his throat.

"What happened?"

"I need your help. Been looking everywhere for you," Jules said with an underlying innuendo.

"I'm here now."

"Good, because we're about to get forty guests who want their fill of turkey."

"You want me to cook?"

"Can you peel potatoes?"

"Well, yeah, but..."

"Hurry up, then," she told him, leading the way to the kitchen. "It's my first year in charge, and I don't want to fuck it up. The Church sends them. Single mothers, fathers who have lost their jobs, that sort of thing. We only charge two dollars a plate. Kids eat free."

He watched as she tied a white apron across her curvy hips. There was a quiet beauty in the way she tried to hide her indifference, but her heart was showing.

"What do you need me to do?"

"Well, I'd take that jacket off first, if I were you. Then you can start with the potatoes," she said, pointing with her knife. "The turkey's already in the oven, but I'm also making baby carrots, peas and mushrooms, homemade cranberry sauce, gravy, and my very own secret recipe stuffing."

Kurt sauntered into the kitchen with a backpack slung over one shoulder. Sifting through it, he pulled out several cans of store-bought gravy.

"What? Don't look at me that way," she told Corelli who was eyeing the canned stuff with disappointment colouring his cheeks.

"Anything else, boss?" Kurt asked, stuffing a raw carrot in his mouth.

"Yeah, can you see if Ol' Mike is up to playing some songs on his banjo?"

"Live music. I dig it. Will do."

"Great. Thanks, Kurt. *Goddamnit,*" she mumbled, "we're running out of time."

Corelli stared at her from the corner of his eye. He saw past her rough, embittered exterior, and plunged deeper to the layers beneath, and even as profanities escaped her lips, it was a beautiful lament.

"We'll get it done."

"I hope so. Ella's coming, too."

He stopped mid-motion, "With her dad?"

"God, no. I'm not stupid, Corelli."

Strangers' voices drifted towards them as guests started to arrive. Jules had decorated the Great Room with Autumn centerpieces on each table. Orange garland was wrapped around the table legs. For a split second in time, Corelli felt at home, and not like a wanderer: a nomad in blue jeans.

"I'll go settle them in," Jules told him, touching his forearm on her way past. An unfamiliar sensation rode up his backbone; one that wasn't linked to desire, but rather, affection.

When Jules returned, she was morose and silent, having wiped the hostess smile from her face. He approached her stealthily, like when his childhood friends had huddled in a corner, giggling, as he gathered the courage to submit to his playground crush with a love note penned in crayon.

"Are you okay?" he asked, bringing her a pot full of peeled potatoes.

Her hands worked overtime, gathering ingredients from the fridge, and doing everything possible to avoid looking at him. Grasping a large knife, she unleashed her negative energy on an onion. "There's a woman out there that reminds me of my mother. You know I used to sit in the shopping cart when I was little just so that it was easier to steal? Mom had me stuff things up my shirt. If we got caught, her plan was always to blame it on me just being a stupid kid. Thing is, we never got caught."

"That guilt belongs to her, though. Not you."

"I guess. There's just all this food in front of me and people out there that are hungry, and...I don't know...." She trailed off, glancing at the wall clock. Its tick was slow, audible. In her mind, the hands were gesticulating wildly. "I thought Ella would be here by now."

"Do you want me to go and get her?"

Jules stopped chopping. The tears welling in her eyes were meant for him, "Thanks, but you've done enough. Who knows what kind of mood that asshole's in?"

He stood next to her, with his back against the counter and his arms crossed over his heart to prevent it from dropping, "We'll go together, then."

"What about all this?" she asked, referring to the un-made feast before her.

"I'll rally the troops. I'm sure between Kurt and Mike, they can figure out how to boil water. It'll only take us Thirty minutes. Twenty, if you can run," he teased, bumping his shoulder into hers.

She turned to look at him. In her eyes, he saw a glimmer of hope. He's seen that look before. That look has been seared in his memory, belonging to all those seeking forgiveness by an unseen Deity.

Her words were definitive.

"Find them."

~

They choked on dust as a truck sped by. Both Jules and Corelli were mute, afraid to voice the thoughts that were tumbling around their heads. There could be no answer, with no question posed.

Upon the wind, he heard his mother's voice as it circled the globe, catching up to him. On a day in 1962, a storm raged, dramatically changing a blue sky to black. She had stood on their front step calling his name. He had heard her muffled cry, but pretended not to, choosing to brave the snow to fulfill some imaginary rite of passage. As the rickety house drew near, his mother's words were amplified: *"Don't come crying to me when you find what you're looking for!"*

"Why are you stopping? We're almost there."

Her cheeks were cherub-red from the exertion of walking at a fast pace. Corelli lit a smoke and took three long drags before tossing it underfoot. "I'll go get her. You wait here."

"How gallant of you, Corelli, but I'm coming with you. Let's go," she said, turning her back on him.

Grabbing her by the forearm, he cautioned her by saying nothing at all.

"Let's go," she repeated, cocking her head towards the house.

He followed her as she ran the length of the driveway. Without hesitating, she knocked three times, hard. Corelli stood next to her with his fists clenched. The red drained from her cheeks. His fist met the door.

"It's Thanksgiving. Maybe they went to see family."

"They don't *have* any family. They don't even own a car."

Jules descended the steps and cupped her hands on the living room window to peer inside. Several cans of beer lined the coffee table, along with an empty bottle of liquor, dead on its side. An ashtray overflowed. Chicken wing bones riddled the space next to the grungy sofa in stark contrast to the picture books that were strewn on the carpet. She imagined her sitting on the floor, escaping into worlds with dragons, fairies, and Prince Charming, borrowing fantasies by the word and hoarding them in her subconscious.

"Well?"

"I don't see them."

"Wait here. I mean it, Jules."

She stood paralyzed, like her dream self, unable to run from impending danger. Her throat constricted, as she thought of Ella living in squalor. In spite of her own impoverished childhood, she was empathetic by nature and was haunted by life's cruelties, like the emaciated visages of starving children in Ethiopia.

The silence unnerved her. She called his name to combat the terror creeping up inside of her, "Corelli!"

A squirrel startled her as it ran up a tree's trunk, manic, and free, and content, *"Goddammit.* Corelli! Answer me!"

Her heart sped at the sound of rustling leaves. Her lips met her crucifix. She willed her legs to move. He stepped forward, grasping her by both arms, "Don't."

"Why? Did you find her?"

[81]

His tortured features gave him away. Furious with God, he was amazed by how quickly repulsion replaced admiration. The lines in his face deepened. The fire in his belly was snuffed out, leaving him with a violent ache.

"Why won't you answer me? Did you *see* them!?"

"Jules...I'm begging you."

"What!? Let me through..."

She struggled in his arms, as he attempted to shield her from the unholy.

"You don't want to see this, Jules!"

"What the fuck are you talking about? Let me go!" she screamed, kicking at his shin and freeing herself.

Corelli stood frozen with his hands on his knees as if praying to his Saviour, but his Saviour wasn't listening. A deathly calm preceded her anguished cry. It echoed endlessly, like the screech of a train whistle. He ran to her, catching her as she fell from the milkcrate that rested beneath the kitchen window, and on the descent, she screamed one syllable repeatedly, *"No! No! No!"*

Inside the kitchenette, a father and daughter were positioned rather comically with their faces in their bowls. An opened bottle of rat poison sat next to the maple syrup, and the light was forever dimmed in a woman's eyes.

A night so dreary,

He, so weary,

Setting out to pray.

The steeple beckons,

His stride, leaden,

Heavily, his fear weighs.

"Oh, priest, forgive me,

See me on knee,

Cursed be this day."

No echo heard,

No holy word,

The priest, he hangs aweigh.

-Cris Corelli's Diary

Ten

The monster wasn't beneath the bed. It was in the mirror, swallowing at all the vile things it wanted to say – choking on bile to make them go away.

"God *damn* you, God."

Leaving the bathroom, Corelli returned to his room, locking himself inside, afraid that someone would come and save him. The floorboards creaked in response to his pacing. He replayed his conversation with the police in his head, revisiting things gruesome on a day that was meant for giving thanks, and praise. Dropping to his knees, he retched, thinking of her and the way she ran into the street towards a speeding car, intent to join Ella. The car had swerved, and as he caught up to her, he was horrified by the look on her face: one of pure, and utter indifference.

He tore at the buttons on his shirt, pounding at his flesh to eradicate the gross affliction eating at his heart. Coming to his feet, he blasted Heavy Metal on the radio to help purge thoughts of self-mutilation. The Bible sat open on the windowsill. Ink swirled together senselessly.

"Fuck you, God," he blasphemed, tearing pages out of the sacred book. "Fuck you."

Beneath the noise disguised as music, he heard pounding. He kicked at the ghetto blaster to silence it. The knocking grew incessant. He walked to the door and placed his fingers over the lock. Through the wood, he spoke in monotone, "Who is it?"

The silence was thick, foreboding.

"Go to hell, then."

The stranger knocked harder.

"Jesus Christ, what!?" he screamed, swinging the door open.

Racoon eyes stared at him; lids swollen from crying. Her smile was the stuff that nightmares are made of.

"Fancy a drink?" she asked, holding up a half-empty bottle of whisky. She glanced at his bare chest before pushing her way inside, uninvited.

She was displaced in his cell. The bed moaned with pleasure as she sat, legs crossed. The bottle met her lips. Corelli couldn't move. He felt the sweat gather at the nape of his neck. His dehydrated lips tingled.

"Close the door."

Hinges squeaked as he secured the lock. The temptation before him tormented him. They were victims in their own right; bonded by mutual suffering.

The alcohol sloshed as she pushed the poison in his direction, making him flinch.

"I won't tell anyone, Corelli."

Admitting defeat, she lowered the bottle, placing it between her thighs. Moonlight filtered through the window, suffusing her in a spotlight, like the one his mother coveted on stage.

"I used to skip classes to go to the beach. Sometimes, I'd bring this shit with me," she said, flicking at the whisky with two fingers. "Mostly, though, I'd just sit in the sand, even when it was raining, and ran my fingers through it for hours."

His legs gave way. He approached the bed and sat behind her with his back against the headboard. Jules shifted her body to face him. They resembled survivors lost at sea, floating on a tiny raft that threatened to overturn.

"You know what's stupid? Eh? That we had to face all that today while other people were stuffing their faces with turkey. Like they don't give a shit about anyone but themselves." Her laugh was vulgar. "A whole Goddamned plane can fall out of the sky, and they'll say, 'Oh, how tragic', before going back to their dinner, or going to sleep, or fucking."

His eyes drifted to her breasts, visible and naked beneath her sheer, white blouse.

"I never forgave him for dying, you know."

"Who are you talking about?"

"Dad," she said, tipping the bottle to cheers a long-dead soldier.

Jules walked to the window with the liquor clutched in one hand. The moon emitted an orange glow. Its pockmarked surface grew beautiful. An epitaph was scripted across the sky. "I already miss her, Corelli."

Sobbing, she collapsed to the floor, bathing in the whisky that flowed from the bottle neck. Her head met her knees. Tears melded with the alcohol. He joined her on the ground, adopting the same position with his knees to his chest, and as Jules caved to the effects of the venom she consumed, Corelli kept a midnight vigil at her side.

"What would happen if I could record your dreams? Would you show me the best parts of yourself? Would I see you skipping from cloud to cloud, or would you be sharing tea with Satan? Defying all logic, I want to see inside your head and discover the ugliest parts of you."

-Cris Corelli's Diary, October 15th, 1985

Eleven

He awoke from his drunken stupor, the sweet taste of syrup on his lips. He leaned over, caressing her delicate curves, lingering on that place of her innocence where she gave herself to him...

Whisky streamed across the uneven floor and flowed into the gaps between the hardwood. Shifting uncomfortably, Corelli groaned. He was propped against the wall with his neck twisted to one side. His bedmate had disappeared sometime in the hollow of the night, leaving him with a protuberant erection that spoke of his longing. She picked at his heart like she would the tiny petals of a Forget-Me-Not. Her absence was palpable.

Coming to his feet, he stretched the kinks out of his weary body. He approached the window, staring dumbly at the world outside. The distinct, flute-like song of a meadowlark pierced the silence. Its yellow breast reminded him of a bedtime story spoken by his father to help thwart nighttime adversaries. It was the story of a man who lived in a humble home, employing rituals to fight off loneliness. He would eat the same meal and read the same book before slumber each night. Then, before he had a chance to bemoan his solitary life, he would rest his head on a pillow filled with shiny, yellow gold.

"If he was rich, why didn't he use his money to buy friends?"

"He's the dream keeper. He's waiting for you," his father told him, handing him a chocolate coin wrapped in gold paper.

Sounds coming from the hallway drifted towards his room. The boarding house was waking, and Corelli could hear Ol' Mike and Kurt's muted voices. Their whispers failed to disguise the macabre. When Corelli and Jules did not return, the two men had cooked and served the Thanksgiving dinner to hungry mouths, to help lighten an impossible burden.

Corelli opened his door and entered the bathroom, ignoring their sympathetic glances. He recalled the times that he had stood at the head of a casket and scrutinized the mourners who hid behind sunglasses to mask not their tears, but rather the unextinguishable joy in their eyes.

He ran the water until it was painfully hot, cleansing his face, arms, and torso, reveling in the burn. He imagined his skin was flammable; his arms scorched, burning to the tendon and bone. His guilt festered deep within his innards, a blight upon his soul.

Turning off the water, he dried himself with his t-shirt, casting it to the side. The tiny window faced east where an Elder tree stood the test of time; its magical properties promising protection for the inhabitants inside a dwelling. Beneath it, he saw her sitting in the leaves, her back to him, drawing upon that magic.

He left the bathroom to dress. His room reeked of booze. Tremoring inside, he buttoned his flannel shirt, and as he thought of the alcohol meeting his lips, his throat constricted with panic. At the dresser, his fears were manifested in an empty brown pill bottle.

"Fuck!"

Throwing the bottle across the room, it bounced off the Bible and rolled towards the sticky pool of alcohol on the floor. God was a jokester.

Corelli laughed, threw on his leather jacket, lit a smoke, and set out to meet his date.

~

"If you're here to stop me, you're wasting your time."

He eclipsed the sun standing in front of her. There was an open bottle of wine nestled between her legs as she sat on the ground in the style of Indians. An untouched plate covered in plastic wrap held gelatinous slices of turkey, baby carrots petrified in butter, and congealed stuffing.

"Can I sit?"

[91]

"Whatever."

The earth was cold beneath him. Leaves were still wet and glistening from the morning's dew. They sat side by side, staring off in the distance where the mist clung on the horizon. Peace reigned somewhere untouchable, just out of reach.

"An angel fell from the sky," she said dreamily. "It swaddled me within its wing, and then left me here. I guess my halo is tarnished."

"Is that a poem?"

"Nah. Just the wine talking."

The top of Jules' lip was stained purple. He glanced at the bottle, half-full.

"Did you get any sleep last night?"

"No. You?"

"No."

She faced him with a barren expression, raising her hand towards him before dropping it to her side. "What was it like?"

"What was what like?"

"Being a priest."

Corelli crushed his smoke in a small pile of wet leaves. She was delving deeper, to his layers embossed with memories of things both barbarous, and benevolent.

"Much like being a doctor, I guess. Except I was supposed to save souls."

"*Supposed* to?"

"I did. And I didn't."

"Way to be cryptic, Corelli," she said, suddenly animated. "Why'd you leave? Or did they fire you?" Wine dribbled down her chin, and before she could stop him, he wiped it away with one thumb.

"I left on my own."

"Why?"

Like a reverse confession, the words were trapped inside of him. Lighting a cigarette, he watched as the smoke circled endlessly, like the thoughts of a madman.

"Not now, Jules."

"Oh, okay," she said sarcastically. "Let's just sit here then, while I get drunk."

"Shit's no good for you," he said, salivating.

She pushed at his shoulder playfully, "You my father now? Speaking of which, what about your old man?"

"Died when I was a kid."

"Well, ain't that a coincidence? How?"

He saw his father before him, standing in the field, holding a guitar case with curves that rivaled those of a woman.

"Went and got himself killed. He was a musician. A greedy one. Or lazy, is more like it. Stole other people's songs. Pissed the wrong guy off, and that was that."

Jules' eyes widened, giving off the illusion that there was life still left inside of her. "Sounds like a country song."

"Yeah. I loved him, though."

"That's sweet, Corelli. Did he sing to you often?"

"He did. Sang to my mother too, but when the words are stolen, even love songs sound indecent."

Jules picked at the label of the wine bottle with ragged nails. The bright red polish was bleeding.

"Fuck love," she said earnestly. "All it's ever done is gotten me in trouble."

He saw her with a protruding belly and could hear the phantom scream of an unborn child. *When the bough breaks, the cradle will fall…*

"Well?"

"Sorry, what did you say?"

"I asked you if a priest can fall in love."

"They didn't take my heart when I signed up, if that's what you mean."

"Yeah? So, you like girls?"

Warmth emanated throughout his thigh where she rested her hand and squeezed. Her boozy gaze bewildered him. Heat rose to his groin. It spread like wildfire, and as his body reacted to her touch, his mind rejected the concept that she desired him. Like 'love', 'sham' is a four-letter word.

Picking up her hand, he placed it in her lap. He stood and walked towards the open field - away from the boarding house, from his life, from her.

He passed his dead dad along the way and tossed him a nickel for all the love songs he didn't play.

One Year Earlier

"It was disgusting. This stunning plate of food that he made with his own hands was disgusting to me."

Father Corelli knew the woman. She liked to sit in the front pew as if God would favour her amongst the throng of sinners. Her spindly arms and legs were hidden beneath layers of clothing. A light fur covered her face and body to help keep her warm. Cheeks concave were dusted with orange blush to mimic a suntan. She wore a giant black bow in her crimped hair, and several black, plastic bracelets on her wrist, to honour the singer whose name was considered a sacrilege to the devoutly religious.

"There must be a sin in there somewhere. Isn't that right, Father?"

"What makes you remorseful?"

Saliva swished around her mouth as she chewed her gum. Annette knew that there were exactly 25 calories in each piece of Hubba Bubba. She allowed herself three a day, tea steeped black with two tea bags, a banana for breakfast, an orange for lunch, and an apple for dinner. Her long sleeves were meant to warm her, as much as they were meant to cover the mysterious bruises on her wrists. She grew sleepy in the confessional.

"Annette?"

"Hmm? Oh, sorry, Father. I don't know. I'm sorry I yelled at him, I guess. I'm sorry that I hurt him."

Father Corelli tried to think if he'd ever seen a man sitting with her at Sunday mass.

"Your husband?"

"He's not my husband. Says he won't marry me... while...while I'm like this. I'm living in sin. Strike two against me," she said, her jaw tightening. "So, anyway, just before coming here, I took that plate of roast beef and tossed it in the trash. Didn't even take one bite. That's when Don went mental."

Judge not, lest ye be judged...

"Did he become violent with you?"

Annette laughed weakly, "That son of a bitch would lose a tickling match. No, he didn't hit me. Let's just say he used unchaste words against me. Said he lived in a brothel. Said he *lives* in a brothel, I mean. Said that he knows what I do when he's not around...whatever that means, since I don't do anything except watch my Soaps all day. Oh, and the *Twenty Minute Workout*. I never miss a day, Father," she said, proudly.

Syllables dissolved before the priest could say something that went against his contract with God. He was God's ears, nothing else. Bowing his head, he recited the words ad nauseum, "Are you sorry for these sins as you recount them now, in the name of..."

[97]

"Wait. I wasn't finished yet. My time's not up, is it?"

"Of course not. I'm sorry," he said, embarrassed. "You may continue."

"Don was drinking that expensive white wine that I hate. Not because it's wine, but because it's expensive, you know? And he buys it anyway. With *our* money. When he started calling me a whore, I could feel it all the way to my toes. It hurt, you know?" she repeated, nervously.

The Autumn sun had set, leaving the Church cold, and vacant of any spiritual presence. In the booth next to him, Annette dozed off.

"You resent him."

"What?" she asked, confused. "Oh. Yeah, that's right. I *do* resent him. When he turned his back, I grapt...I *grabbed* his wine glass and smashed it against the dining room table like I was some sort of mobster or something. The bottom broke off, leaving just the stem. I..."

"What, Annette?"

"I...I jabbed it in his eye. *That's...that's...strike three,*" she whispered, clutching at her heart.

The wind howled. Beneath it, God had delivered His breathy verdict.

"For unlawful carnal knowledge."

- Cris Corelli's Diary

Twelve

The sun was sleeping. Corelli spent the day wandering around town, avoiding eye contact with the townspeople, who, in his mind, took on sinister qualities; their intentions malicious. He stopped at *The Mousetrap* for a Coke and French Fries, hoping to chat with Mabel, but she had failed to show up for her daily tea. He had scribbled a note on a napkin and asked Jonah to deliver it to the blind woman.

"How the hell is she supposed to read this? Through osmosis?"

"Your eyes work, don't they?"

Jonah read aloud, "'The greatest expressions need only a few words. Your friend, Cris.' *That's deep. Enjoy the fries."*

At a dusty antique shop that was nestled between a bakery and an apothecary, Corelli had chanced upon a collection of poetry by A. A. Smith, circa 1884. Its dull brown cover was engraved with gold lettering reminding him of a mannequin sporting a diamond necklace.

The inscription inside had faded with time:

To My Dear Sister Maggie,

With Affection,

December 25th, 1886.

The penmanship was archaic, and in the dips and swirls of consonants and vowels, he imagined an elementary life; straightforward, and uncomplicated in its resolve.

A man older than Ol' Mike had greeted him at the register. He exuded charm, despite his scarred face and mismatched attire. Like a book, the man quietly asked to be judged by what was inside.

Carrying the collection of poetry beneath his arm, Corelli entered the boarding house that was devoid of any human life. The silence was overwhelming, and he tossed his boots against the wall to challenge the voices in his head that spoke of morbid things.

He walked towards the spiraling staircase, stopping abruptly at the sound of a crash as if a robber were searching for the elusive treasure. Depositing her gift on the third stair, he made his way towards Jules' room, where, buried beneath the sound of glass shattering, he heard her gut-wrenching cries.

A cold sweat covered his body. The shadowy remains of a man and his daughter scaled the walls in the darkened hallway.

[101]

Corelli jiggled the door handle and slapped at the wood with an open palm until his hand stung.

"Jules. It's me. Let me in."

The sweat pooled at the small of his back. He shrugged his leather jacket off and dropped it to the floor. It fell with its sleeves extended, eerily resembling a crime scene chalk outline.

"Jules!"

A deathly calm preceded the sound of furniture hitting the floor. Her screams petrified him. Inside her room, Jules was buying time, using tears to bribe the Reaper.

"Fuck…Open the *Goddamn* door!

Giving up, he ran back towards the foyer, threw on his boots, and headed outside where he circumvented the ghosts that masqueraded around the property as humans; their fleshly imprints visible in the mud.

He stumbled over a tree root that protruded from the earth; its scraggly limbs inched towards him like the emaciated hand of his mother. Beneath him, the ground thumped an irregular beat in the manner of a dying heart, seeping its last bits of love.

A yellow glow led him to her open window where he hurriedly crawled inside, extending one hand in front of him in defense.

"I'm only here to help."

Her vacant stare morphed into a maniacal one. She stepped around the debris on the floor, grabbed his hand and forced him on his knees.

"Pray. I need you to pray. I don't think He'll listen to me, Corelli." She knelt by his side, still holding his hand. "Tell Him. Tell Him I'm sorry!"

The booze lingered on the air as she breathed. Her hair was partially up, leaving long, unkempt strands that shielded her face, causing her to look gaunt, and frail.

"What are you waiting for? You want to help? Pray for me!"

"Stop it, Jules," he said, releasing her hand. He stood and surveyed the small room, destroyed by her wrath. A shattered mirror rested before her and in it, he saw her demons.

"What? What are you saying? Are you saying you won't help me?"

"You're drunk."

"So what? So *what*, Corelli? What does that mean? That I'm unworthy of forgiveness?"

Vinyl records riddled the floor, along with horror novels, strings of multi-coloured fake pearls, a Lava lamp that emitted rainbow hues, and her dresser that had spilled its guts.

"What exactly are you sorry for? For this?" he asked her, thrusting one hand outward.

[103]

Crickets sang a symphony, melodious and unwelcomed. Slowly, she came to her feet and faced him like a blushing bride who stands before her groom.

"I…"

"What are you sorry for!?"

"I…I don't fucking know, okay!? For being born!"

She approached the bed where she had left her bottle of liquor. Corelli snatched it from her grasp and hid it behind his back. Without it, the monster within was untamed.

"Give that to me."

"No. That's enough."

"Give it to me!" she screamed, encircling his waist with her arm.

He raised the bottle towards the ceiling, offering it to God.

"No, Jules."

Spent, she sat on the side of the mattress, a wounded expression on her face, "What are you even doing here, then? Eh? First, you won't pray for me, and now you…"

"I'm saving you from yourself."

Doubling over, she laughed perversely, "You are saving *me*?" she asked staring up at him. "Who is saving *you*, Corelli? You were there. You saw, too. Her face…" she said, bursting into tears, "…her little face."

[104]

Jules' chin met her chest. She held her breath, capturing it within her lungs, intent to live. Like a wind-up toy, she whipped her head in his direction. "It's all your fault, you know. If you hadn't gone to see that asshole the first time…if you had only let it be, like I asked you to…I hope you're proud of yourself, Corelli," she said, a bitter smile on her lips.

Acid bubbled in his stomach. There was nowhere left to run. In her words, he heard perilous truths, and beneath his hand, he held an elixir. Forsaking some made-up moral code, he stepped out of his body and watched from a distance as the liquor met his lips.

"Tastes good, doesn't it?"

Sucking on the bottle was like sucking on his mama's breast. Amber liquid washed away the guilt. He coughed uncontrollably and spat on the floor, envisioning a hole burned into the carpet – a chasm to hell.

"Easy, there," she said, extending her hand.

He relinquished the booze and sat next to her, trembling with delight. Colours grew bright, and behind his lids, his tears evaporated.

"I guess we're both sorry," he said, placing his head in his hands.

"Hey. Hey, don't do that." Jules grasped his chin, forcing him to look at her. "Why'd you come here, Corelli? Where are you going?"

He licked the whisky from his lips, savouring it. "The truth is, I have no place to go. I'm that guy you see leaning on a lamp post in the middle of the night. There's...there's nothing, and no one."

"We're both orphaned, then," she said, handing him the bottle. She watched as he drank freely, searching for salvation. "I need you, Corelli. Here. With me."

The crickets ceased their song. Silence lingered. She adopted a look of purity, beckoning him by saying nothing at all.

Her admission gave him power. His desire fueled his actions. Taking her hand, he placed it on his thigh, just as she had in the field, underneath their tree.

He stroked her cheek, wiping at the makeup that had melted beneath her tears. His thumb caressed her bruised lips. He tasted her, gently at first, and then he took her head in his hands and devoured her mouth, eating all the words she had yet to say.

In the near darkness of the room, her crucifix shone a warning. He was in a showdown with Jesus.

"What's wrong?"

"Nothing," he said, tossing the pendant behind her back.

Colour rose to her cheeks. They breathed in tandem; two people seeking absolution in one another. Guiding her on the bed, he explored her long, lean body.

She found his belt and slid her hand between his taut abdomen and the fabric of his jeans, watching as his face contorted into something alien.

He reveled in her sultry murmurs as one hand enveloped her full breast. He undressed her slowly, marveling at her beauty, torturing her. Naked, her heart visible, she writhed on the bed, aching for him.

"Please..."

He freed himself from his jeans, moaning without shame as she found him, wrapping her fingers around him, pleasuring him.

"Cris...*please*..." she whispered.

He raised his body over hers, and kissed her mouth, her neck, her chest – thrusting his fingers inside of her, over and over. She pushed his hand away, arching her back, and as he enveloped her fully, he took her to some other realm, void of sadness, and pain.

Deep inside of her, he found nirvana.

"When we were eleven years old, we pledged our 'forever love' by wearing various coloured beads on our shoelaces. The red ones were the most coveted. One day, my lace broke and the beads flew in different directions. I never did find my version of 'forever'."

-Cris Corelli's Diary, October 16th, 1985

Thirteen

"There's an old bridge just south of here. The wooden kind. If you look closely enough, there are names etched in the railing."

They resembled mummies lying next to each other with their hands over their bellies, acting as if nothing had happened. The early morning darkness was deceiving, tricking them into believing that it was still the dead of night.

"Lovers?"

"Survivors."

He shifted his body towards her and leaned on his elbow. She looked ethereal in the dimness of the room; the monster subdued.

"Is your name among them?"

"Yeah," she said, staring at the ceiling. "I go back there often. Sometimes, I stare into the murkiness, and can see them resting in watery graves. There's nothing really there. I can still see them, though."

A gust of icy air washed over them, chilling him to the bone. Or maybe it was her words that made his blood run cold.

"You'll see my hair, spread just right / My arms and legs, in dance delight / Weightless as a Summer breeze / Do not cry, for I'll be free."

She faced him with eyes wide open. "That's exactly what I meant. Who wrote that?"

"I made it up."

"Just now?" she asked, moving to her side.

"Yes."

"You're full of surprises, aren't you, Corelli? They teach you how to write poetry at priest school?"

His fingers met her cheek. He rose from bed and searched for his crumpled Levi's. Finding his smokes, he slid back underneath the covers, sitting up against the headboard. She mimicked him, letting the sheet fall from her breasts. The parts she wanted hidden, resided inside of her.

"My dad's influence, I guess. Songs are pretty much poetry set to music."

Lighting a cigarette, he handed it to her. Its orange glow reminded him of a hearth with burning embers, where the smoldering ashes of naughty children burned eternally. It was an ancient Nun's Tale rivaling *The Brothers Grimm*.

"I can't write. Can't sing, or dance, either. Can't do anything except mess things up," she said, handing the smoke back to him.

She swung her legs over the edge of the bed, head lowered in silence.

"That's not true, Jules."

"Isn't it? There are things you don't know," she said, talking to the wall. "Things you don't want to know."

"I think most things in life are an illusion."

"What makes it worth living, then?" she asked over her shoulder. She stood unsteadily; her body wracked by grief.

"Where are you going?"

"To make breakfast," she said, pulling down a silk robe from a hook and wrapping it around herself. "I have a boarding house to run. Make sure you're gone before I get back."

She disappeared into the hallway, putting an end to their forbidden tryst. As the sun rose, her aura lingered; charred red, like the embers.

~

He sat on the floor, leaning against the foot of the bed with his legs stretched before him. Despite his grumbling stomach, he didn't eat. After a brief trip to town, he holed himself up in his room, sequestering his thoughts, lassoing them.

Minutes turned into hours. A depleted wine bottle sat at his side, and he was well on his way to draining another; the booze successfully euthanizing his feelings of euphoria.

He could still feel her. He could feel the warmth of her insides. He could feel her breath on his neck. He could feel the knife in his back.

[111]

He had reconciled with His Father above, only to be struck down by an immoral temptress. A day, long forgotten, resurfaced in his mind. He had been alone, dusting pews before service. A woman had entered the church, dressed in the way of a harlot.

"May I help you?"

"Just here to pray, Father."

"Please, feel free."

"I won't be long, if you'd like some company when I'm through."

"I'm sorry. I don't think I understand."

"I cannot change who I am. I can only show the Lord my true self."

Coming to his feet, Corelli turned on the radio, sifting through the static until words became clear. Someone sang a song of unrequited love, like a eulogy spoken in his honour.

Taking a swig from the bottle, he heard demons screeching, ridiculing him for his weakness.

"Fuck you," he said out loud, raising his libation in a cheer.

"That's pretty unchivalrous of you, Corelli."

He spun abruptly to see her standing at the threshold of his room, leaning on the doorframe with one arm raised above her, seeking admiration from an audience of one. Her black, leather, micro-mini hugged her hips. A baby blue halter top barely covered her navel. The harsh lines around her eyes were crudely drawn, and on her lips, painted scarlet, she wore a suggestive smile.

"I see you started the party without me."

Jules closed the door behind her, securing the lock. She deposited a full bottle of something clear on his nightstand, and approached him, moving like the flame from the candle that burned on the windowsill.

"I thought I'd see you for lunch. Or dinner."

"Wasn't hungry."

She stopped mere inches from his face. Liquor perfumed the air between them.

"You mad at me, Corelli?"

Her fingers met his hair. They danced across his face, his neck, moving towards his chest. He restrained her, squeezing her wrist, and holding her hand against his broken heart.

"Are you here to use me? Like you did last night?"

Her eyes changed colour. In them, he saw a temporary respite. "I didn't use you. We used each other," she said, pulling away.

The empty wine bottle on the floor was like an invitation. She sat on his bed. One leg was crossed over the other, and then at the ankles: The Serpent in human form.

"Is that what you think I did? Use you?"

"What else would you call it? Anyway, it doesn't matter. I came to tell you something. I saw her today," she said, unscrewing the cap off the Sambuca bottle.

"What are you talking about?"

"Ella. She came to tell me to stop crying. But I can't. I can't stop, Corelli." Her tears fell quietly, and as she brushed them away, he saw his mother before him – the damsel in distress. "Come. Come sit with me. I brought you a gift."

He stood motionless, fighting a quiet battle in his head, afraid of a little girl's ghost.

"Please."

Walking a few feet towards her, he snatched the Sambuca from her hand and chugged from it, trying to tame an unquenchable thirst.

"Where'd you see her? Ella, I mean."

"In the kitchen. I was doing dishes, and there she was. You believe me, don't you?" Jules took the wine from his hand, leaving him with the Sambuca.

He fell on the bed, deliberately leaving a space between them.

"Ghosts aren't real."

Disgust shadowed her features. "I'm telling you that I saw her. You're the spiritual one. Isn't the soul supposed to live on?"

[114]

A woman dressed in period garb rustled her skirts. He squeezed his eyes shut to make his mother retreat heavenward.

"You saw a vision. Your mind's playing tricks on you. Nothing else," he said, taking a drink. Walking to the window, he felt the floor sway beneath his feet. Jasmine permeated the air –reminding him of his childhood, his mother's signature scent.

"Jesus Christ, why can't you just let me have this one thing!?"

She joined him at the window and stole a glance at their reflection, hoping to see a third figure in the pane. For once, she wished she believed in fairy tales.

"What's with this?" he asked, rubbing the sticky goo from her lips. "Eh? A mask? Who are you hiding from?"

She smudged the last of her lipstick across her cheek and glared at him; her heart swelling with anger. "Go to hell, Corelli."

"Cheers to that," he said, hitting the bottle. He placed it next to the candle, causing a colourful prism to emit from the ethanol.

"I shouldn't have come here."

"Then go."

"You're a bastard."

"You know what they say. Takes one to know one."

She struck him, sullying what was left of their union. Corelli lifted his head to see her standing in front of him, unremorseful -- like the black sheep of his congregation who seek pardon too late. Emboldened by his demons, he took her arm and ushered towards the door where she twisted herself in his arms, ready to repent.

"I'm sorry," she said through garbled tears. "I am. I shouldn't have hit you. I just…I'm scared. I'm scared for myself…for you. I don't know what's happening to me. I can't breathe. I can't breathe anymore. Please, forgive me."

Forgive me, Father…

He caught her as her legs gave way, sending her to the floor like a rag doll. Picking her up, he gently placed her on the bed. The mattress swallowed her feeble body. He brushed the hair from her eyes and sat on the edge, his back towards her to ward off temptation. Her cold hand encircled his arm, and as she pulled him down with her, they slipped into an erotic purgatory where they awaited final judgement.

~

She slept with her head on his chest. Moving her onto her back, he rose from bed and slid on his boxers. The hallway was as cold as a refrigerator's belly. His head ached and his innards gurgled.

Inside the bathroom, he leaned on the wall, relieving himself. Terror engulfed him as the white bulb radiated shades of red. Poison shot through his veins. Vomit spewed from his mouth. He stumbled backwards, hitting the tub, sending him spiralling down the rabbit hole. Her singsong filled his ears: *Father Cris! Father Cris! Father Cris!*

The apparition smiled; cheeks chubby, and smeared with chocolate.

"I have met my executioner.

He resides in the decaying body of an eight-year old girl."

-Cris Corelli's Diary, October 17th, 1985

Fourteen

"I'll see you tonight?" She kissed him softly. It was a mad sort of love; the kind of game that adults play, tinged by sadness.

Closing the door behind her, he hurried to the dresser to unearth his Bible that he had hastily buried. The book felt foreign between his hands. Yellowed pages crackled beneath his fingertips. He flipped at them furiously; his eyes desperately scanning the words. He envisioned himself ten years earlier, standing at the pulpit, feeling displaced in the House of Worship. Parishioners had gawked at him as they would the circus side-show freak. Whispers had swept through the crowd. Judgements had been made. Beneath his robes, he was a mere mortal.

As the verse came into focus, Corelli recited it out loud: "Job 14:12: 'So man lieth down, and riseth not: till the heavens be no more, they shall not awake, nor be raised out of their sleep'."

His heart was idling as his fear dissipated. Logic annulled thoughts of the undead. He had been seduced by the alcohol that still coursed through his veins; deceived by his own culpability surrounding Ella's death.

Feeling claustrophobic, he grabbed his leather jacket and left the boarding house. On the opposite side of the street, he stared at the building that held a hundred years of memories within its red-bricked walls. The hands on his watch sped counterclockwise. He could see workers dressed in overalls, and wearing flat caps laying brick, and roof shingles. He saw a woman donning velvet bloomers pull up the dirt drive on an oversized Schwinn bicycle to deliver lunch to her beau; offerings nestled in a pail covered in a crisp cotton towel. He watched as they shared a phantom kiss, laced with longing, and a love so pure, he almost looked away.

A Polaroid of his own life materialized before his eyes. He was six, filling a little brown bag with penny candy. The orange jujubes were his favourite. He was enticed by their fiery colour, and when the burly man behind the counter dropped a handful of free candy into his bag, he felt like a King for the rest of the day, feasting on sugar, and making up fantasies, as all little boys should.

A commercial vehicle drove by, breaking his trance. Ghosts retreated on the wind. The woman on the bicycle rode past him, her body fading into smoky wisps. The boarding house morphed into its current state – no longer pristine, as it was in its infancy.

He walked towards the wooded area with an old familiar tune on his lips that spoke of lonely hearts, and second chances. Buried beneath the rustling of leaves, a little girl's restless spirit whispered the chorus.

~

"Get your coat. We're going out."

He was an inadequate suitor, reserving sweet talk and curbing his tongue.

"Where are we going?"

"Out of here."

"Hang on," she said, leaving him standing in the doorway.

Like a voyeur, he watched as she pulled her sweater over her head and put on her red, sheer, tunic with only her black bra underneath. She ran her brush through her long hair and placed giant gold hoops in her earlobes. At the closet, she grabbed a jacket and met him at the door, prim, and unlike herself.

"Ready," she said, threading her arm through his.

Outside, Corelli lit a smoke and flipped the collar on his leather jacket. He stared up at the sky, dotted with millions of stars that looked like they were put there by a sewer's needle. His breath was visible as he exhaled.

"You sure you're warm enough?"

"Why? Are you going to offer me your jacket?"

He gave her a sidelong glance but didn't answer her. His brain worked overtime as they walked two blocks in silence. Scanning the road before him, he caught a glimpse of himself when he was in third grade. The kids used to tease him relentlessly. They threw sticks, as well as stones, and barbs that were meant to sting. They liked to call him

"Chicken Little" to mock his stature. He grew into a big man's shoes, and when he traded in his jeans for a Catholic vestment, he felt empowered.

Turning a corner, they could see the bar's façade. Its plain wood exterior made it resemble a secluded cabin in the woods. Two men straddled their motorcycles, drinking from bottles hidden underneath brown paper bags. Their vulgar ramblings were drowned beneath the shrill of a train whistle.

Corelli held the door open for Jules. *The Mousetrap* was sparsely occupied. A lone woman was setting up her equipment on a small stage at the front of the room. A chalkboard menu advertised Thursday Night Wing Night at 10 cents each. The lights were dimmed, and he chose a tall table for two against the far wall, furthest from the stage and from the main door.

"You're not going to pull my chair out for me?"

He looked at her with a blank expression.

"I'm kidding, Corelli, relax," Jules said, placing her jacket over the back of her chair. "Are you still angry or something?"

"No."

"Could have fooled me."

Jonah approached them with a towel draped over one arm mimicking a waiter in a Michelin Star restaurant.

"Let me guess. A Coke?"

"Whisky on ice. Make it a double."

"I'll have one too," Jules said.

"Now we're talking. Comin' right up."

She helped herself to his cigarettes. He noticed that her hands were shaking, and that her eyes were focused on Jonah as he worked behind the bar.

"Did you have a drink today?"

"What the fuck kind of question is that?" she asked, glaring at him. "Did you invite me here to interrogate me?"

"You're right. Sorry."

"Yeah, well, you should be."

Jonah returned with two rock glasses holding amber liquid. "No ice," he said, setting them down. "Machine's broken. Cheers." He stole a glance at Jules before walking away mumbling something beneath his breath.

The singer entered into a slow rendition of *Sweet Dreams*. Her melodic, soulful voice was calming.

"I love *The Eurythmics*. You know I've never even been to a concert?" She picked up her glass and clinked the side of his before indulging in a drink. "What's the last concert you've been to?"

"Does Midnight Mass count?"

"Funny. Wait, are you telling me that you've never been to one either?"

"Not a one."

"That's sad. We're a couple of sad human beings, Corelli."

"I'll drink to that."

Studying him, she tried to decipher who the man behind the cloth was, and decided that he was too striking to have dedicated himself to a life of celibacy.

"What drove you to drink? I mean, if you want to talk about it."

"I don't want to talk about it."

"Okay. Then tell me," she said, pausing seductively. "Have you ever been in love?"

She gathered her hair in her hands and twisted it at the nape of her neck. He could feel his heart pound through his shirt. Love, to him, was not something concrete, stable, and nestled within the confines of a white picket fence. It was a word, a caress, a stolen kiss.

"Time kind of got away from me. I know what it is, though."

"How do you know what it is?" she asked, snuffing out her cigarette.

"I think we all do. I mean, in our own way. I knew what I was sacrificing when I dedicated my life to God."

"And was it worth it?"

"I'm sitting here with you, aren't I?" He shot her a rare smile, genuine, and warm. "What about you? What does 'love' mean to you?" he asked, draining his glass.

[124]

"Tyler Peeke."

"Is that the man who…?"

"No," she quickly said. "He was my best friend growing up. We used to sneak away with a stack of his dad's *Life* Magazines and imagine ourselves somewhere else. His parents were rich doctors, but he was more like me. A rebel, I guess you'd say. Sometimes, he'd bring me leftovers. Exotic things, like venison and rabbit. He took care of me."

"Is that what it is to you? Being saved?"

"Being accepted, warts and all."

He nodded knowingly, "Yeah. Most people think that priests are gods. Not guilty of anything. That we're untouchable, or invincible. It's exhausting, trying to live up to that. To be someone you're not."

"You're preaching to the choir, preacher."

Her brown eyes moistened. They radiated a transcendental quality. She had already lived a thousand lives. Wiping at them, she stood from her chair and picked up their empty glasses. "I need money."

"He'll be back soon."

"No. I want to go. Give me some money, please. I'll get two more and pay the tab."

"You didn't finish your story. What happened to Tyler?" he asked, handing her a twenty-dollar bill.

Sighing hard, she put a period on that part of her life, "Went to some fancy school out of province. Didn't even say good-bye. Left me his Goddamn magazines, though."

The air grew thick with smoke and dissipated. He watched her as she shook her hair loose, letting it cascade down her back. A man wearing a Stetson standing next to her spoke in her ear. She smiled up at him. He signaled Jonah, raising two fingers in the air. Jonah saluted him and poured two shots of something dark. Glasses kissed. Jules' lips moved and she nudged the stranger in the shoulder, bumping her hip against his. He laughed heartily, devouring her with his eyes as she walked away.

Her flaunting made Corelli seethe.

"Cheers," she said, bringing back their drinks.

"You were flirting with that man."

"So? Are you jealous?"

He swung his head back, draining half his glass.

"You *are* jealous."

A group of revelers vacated their table to dance on a sunken dance floor. Bodies collided, swaying drunkenly. He was fixated on the party, to avoid looking at her.

"Hey."

He turned his head and stuffed both hands deep in his pockets, clenching them out of view.

"What?"

Leaning over the small table, she tempted fate, pushing the boundaries, and playing him like a pawn, "Do you want to punish me, Corelli?"

"Try me, Jules."

She sat back and crossed her lean legs. A smirk lingered on her full lips.

The song ended.

The party was over.

∼

"Mother called this morning."

He sat against the headboard. Cigarette smoke drifted around them in waves. She rested her head on his belly, relishing his touch as his fingers traced the outline of her bottom, reddened by a firm hand. They had made love tenderly, both aware of the fragility of life; hearts thumping like Poe's decapitated corpse.

"I assumed…"

"That she's dead? She's not. She's just dead to me."

He placed the smoke near her lips. Ash fell from its tip as she exhaled. She flicked at it mindlessly, like when she was a child and dismembered ants' bodies, never really deriving pleasure from the action. She had hidden her grisly compulsion, burying tiny carcasses in potted plants.

"She hurt you."

[127]

"She hurt everybody. Calls every six months like clockwork…whenever she runs out of money. I never give her any. Somehow, she thinks things will be different the next time she calls."

Jules flipped onto her back. She reached her hand towards his face to caress the stubble on his cheek, and extract words from lips.

"Mine wasn't around much when I was growing up. It was like she blamed me for dad dying."

"You were just a kid. You didn't kill him."

"I know. She needed an outlet for her anger. I was an easy target."

Jules sat up, crossing her legs underneath her. They were bathed in the different colours being emitted by the Lava Lamp: cartoon characters, come to life. Reaching towards her nightstand, she grabbed a skinny cigarette and lit it. The effects of the joint were instantaneous. She grew mellow, fatigued.

"Tell me about the church," she said, offering him the joint.

"What do you want to know?"

"Are you scared? That maybe you pissed God off?"

She waited as Corelli indulged in the drug. He pinched the joint between his fingers and placed it in the ashtray next him. "Where'd you get that shit?"

"Kurt. Kid is good for something. So? You and God still friends?"

"Part of the reason I left, is that I don't believe in Him anymore," he said, caressing her hand with one thumb.

"Jesus. What the hell happened to make you lose your faith?"

He stared at her, silent.

"Oh. I get it," she said, taking her hand back. "The thing that you don't ever want to talk about." She raised her knees to her chest and hugged them. "What's the big secret? Why won't you talk to me?"

He left her sitting alone and approached her window, unclothed, and emotionally bankrupt.

"When I left, and boarded that train, it felt more like home than the church ever did." He spoke to his own reflection in the glass, afraid to look at her. "It was like I was joining the other lost souls who refused to disembark. Like a mass exodus, except we had nowhere to go."

"What made you stop here?"

"I don't know," he said, turning his head, "you?"

"You're high," she teased. "You didn't know I was here."

He grinned at her, and returned to bed, "I used to think I was running away."

"And now?"

"I feel like I'm running towards something."

[129]

"Like Ricky," she said, staring off into the distance.

"Who is Ricky?"

"My brother. The one who died. He was chasing the dream. Thought he could outsmart the bad guy and make it rich."

"He didn't, I take it."

"No," she said, facing him. "He was broke. Owed a bunch of money. Nowhere really to hide. He escaped with the bottle, instead. Outran life for a while, but his liver killed him before the bad guy could."

"I'm sorry, Jules."

She shrugged, defeated by her own sad story. "I'm going to the kitchen. Do you want some water?"

"Sure."

Picking up his flannel shirt from the end of the bed, she stepped into the hallway. Only then, did she drape the garment around her shoulders.

Corelli rested his head against the wall and closed his eyes for a solitary moment of reflection, juggling memories bristling in his mind of dead fathers, and absent mothers, and of the Rickys of the world who worship false idols.

The air shifted. He felt her breath on his face, hot, and dense.

"What did you forget?" he asked, opening his eyes.

The smell of death filled the room. His scream froze before him. Crippled by fear, he held a dead woman's gaze. Caked in blood, and pus, and crud, Irwin Trade's mother stared back, smiling sweetly.

One Month Earlier

"Bless me, Father, for I have sinned. It has been one week since my last confession."

"For it is with your heart that you believe and are justified, and it is with your mouth that you profess your faith and are saved."

Corelli mimicked Father Stevens as he called upon the Father, Son, and Holy Ghost. Through the lattice work, the man's face resembled a checkerboard.

"Vodka still lingers on my breath."

"Did you consider attending the meeting, Cris?"

"Mom needed me. She was in a lot of pain. The worst I've seen. I couldn't leave her."

A baby's cry filled the Church. A mother's whisper silenced it.

"I'm sorry," Father Stevens said.

"I am too. I'm sorry for many things. I…" Corelli lost control of his emotions. His arms were weak, having carried his mother to the sunroom where she felt most at peace. They resembled Michelangelo's Pietà, in reverse. "The most horrifying sound is not a full-fledged scream, Father. It's a whimper. A whimper coming from someone too sick to scream, the blood curdling like spoiled milk in their lungs."

Men in masks had signed her death certificate and sent her home to die.

"What makes it worse I think, is that she used to belt out words to an enthralled audience. She was loved. She was vibrant, and so very talented. I hated her for that. I hated that she was loved. They took her from me, you know. The adoring fans."

Father Stevens shifted uncomfortably, "You should honour your…"

"Don't you think I know that!? I know the fucking commandments. I know what He's thinking too, and I don't care anymore, Father. I really don't. All that matters is…" He trailed off, unwilling to speak the final words. He wasn't ready. Not yet.

The baby wailed.

"I remember when I was a kid. I used to hide her cigarettes. This was after we buried dad. We learned about cancer in school. Mom hit me. Said they were expensive. Said I was too young to know anything. I cried that day. Just as she was crying last night."

The scent of Frankincense was intense.

"She grew frightened last night. She said she was seeing him. She said he was still handsome, like the day they married. I had to spew the token words to comfort her. Some sanctimonious bullshit."

"Cris…"

He clasped his hands tighter. Tighter.

[133]

"She said that she couldn't take it anymore…she said…"

His ears bled.

"Someone shut that baby up!"

A mother hurried towards the vestibule.

"How does 'love' differ from 'hate', Father? Eh? Aren't they the same? Aren't they both laced in fear? Are we not seeking acceptance either way? I accept that she hated me in the moment, but I did it because I love her…and I'm scared that she doesn't know I do."

"Did *what*, son?"

Corelli shook his head, back and forth, back and forth, back and forth. He pounded on the wall between them, harder, and harder. Sobs filled the small space; heart-wrenching cries that could wake the dead.

"She kept begging for mercy. She was begging for it to stop."

"For *what* to stop?"

"She wanted *me* to stop. *I smothered her.* I smothered my mother."

"Underneath a splintered moon, the

Keeper of Souls stands erect in his coach.

His scythe glints in the darkness.

His horses neigh in greeting."

-Cris Corelli's Diary, October 18th, 1985

Fifteen

Thunder boomed to announce a brewing storm. He awoke alone, tangled in damp sheets. Her voice had lulled him to sleep. In his dreams, her lips moved, but there was no message of love. She was a faceless creature, and he screamed, pleading with an uncaring deity to help him wake from the nightmare.

Hurrying downstairs, he found her in the Great Room, wiping tables. She looked at him briefly. Annoyance was swatched across ruddy cheeks. "Where the fuck did you go last night?"

"There's…something I had to do. I didn't want to keep you up."

She stopped wiping and threw the cloth on the table. Facing him, she adopted a look bordering on disdain, "At two in the morning?"

His smile lines had deepened overnight. Mrs. Trade's odour filled his nose, rancid, and layered with dolor.

"Listen, Jules," he said, holding her by the elbows, "we have to get out of here. Away from this place."

"What the hell are you talking about?"

Letting her go, he raked his hand through his hair, unsure of how to relay the kind of story he's only ever read about in horror novels. He sat in one of the chairs, pulling one out for her. The lights flickered. The storm intensified.

She sat with her hands clasped, reminding him of a little girl expecting a reprimand.

"I...have you seen her again? After the first time?"

"Who?"

"Ella," he said, swallowing hard.

"Yeah," she admitted. "I didn't tell you because you already think I'm crazy. Why are you asking?"

"I've seen her too. And I saw..."

"You saw her!? What did she say? Who else did you see?"

He stood abruptly, sending his chair to the floor, and paced in circles; an endless trip to nowhere.

"Goddammit, Corelli."

He froze. The words were like a child's joke on his lips, "I saw a parishioner's dead mother. Last night. When you went for water. I don't know what's happening, but it's not safe here, Jules."

Slowly, she came to her feet. Rain pelted the roof, drowning out his voice in her head, begging her to run.

"No. You said it yourself. Ghosts aren't real."

She picked up the chair and resumed wiping the already clean table. His hand encircled her wrist. "I'm not being paranoid. I saw them."

"No!" She said, freeing herself from his grasp. She leaned on the table, bracing herself. "If I believe you," she said, her head bowed, "it would be the end of me."

[137]

He tried to seize time, to steady it, and let all things heinous tumble into a void. A deafening boom portended disaster.

"We can leave, though. Start somewhere new. Leave the Goddamn ghosts behind. The guilt…"

She rattled the chair in front of her before meeting his eyes, "I can't leave!"

Zebra and Lion Papier-mâché circled over her head. A phantom hand rocked an empty crib.

"Because of the baby."

"What baby?"

"I know, Jules."

"Know what? Are you insane?"

"Forgive us our trespasses," he whispered, struggling to keep his composure.

"What *fucking* baby, Corelli?"

"The miscarriage. I know about the miscarriage."

Her face went ashen. Rage overtook her. She raised her hand towards him in punishment, and for a fraction of a second, he believed he deserved it.

"Don't," he said, pushing her arm to the side. "I'm sorry," he said, holding her to his heart. "I'm so sorry that happened to you."

"*Let* go of me."

"Jules."

"Let me go!"

He released her, ashamed of his inability to console her. Her footsteps resounded through the Great Room as she ran towards the foyer. He followed her, running down the front steps, into the storm.

Her tears melded with angry waters, "It was my fault!" she screamed, competing with the howling wind; words lost, floating endlessly, *"It was my fault."*

She fell to the mud, on her knees, gutted by her sorriness. Vivid images flooded his brain, of churchgoers resting on kneelers, revering the King of Kings, betraying Him in their smutty minds.

Descending to the earth, he held her, protecting her from herself, and from Lucifer as he stood behind her watching the scene with a despicable grin on his ungodly face.

~

Barricaded inside his room, he read poetry to her from the antique book he purchased, filling her ears with amorous murmurings. Stanzas went unacknowledged; his voice became unfamiliar. The vice clamped on his heart as remembrance registered in her eyes.

"I wanted a girl," she said. "Like Ella."

He kissed the top of her head and slid his arm out from underneath her. Her empty stare was worse than any tirade.

[139]

"I'll be right back. Have to piss," he said, in an effort to maintain normalcy. The gap between two worlds was threatening to close, careening them into the pit where the damned go to burn.

In the hallway, he leaned against the wall, eyes closed, challenging the ghosts that lurked in the shadows to take him, and leave Jules alone. A menacing figure emerged. It was his own doppelganger; his conscience come to life.

Making his way down the hall, he stopped in front of Kurt's door and knocked quietly.

"Hey, man. What's up?"

Corelli peered inside the empty room. Two large duffel bags sat on the floor. "Are you leaving?"

"Yeah," Kurt said, opening his door wide. "Old man threatened to cut me off if I don't go work for him. Sucks, but Winter's coming anyway. You don't look so good."

"Listen," Corelli said, ignoring the comment. "Jules isn't…she isn't feeling well. I was hoping maybe you'd have something. Ease the pain?" Stuffing his hand in his jeans, he offered the young man a five-dollar bill.

"Is she okay? I know she was pretty torn up about that little kid. Fucking asshole deserved it, but not the kid."

Corelli saw the swine's form bulging inside a black body bag, and for an instant, he felt at peace.

"She's hurting."

[140]

"I get it. You'll need something stronger than weed," Kurt said, closing the door. He picked up one of the bags and placed it on the stripped bed. "One good thing about having a rich daddy," he said, pulling out a vial holding a gram of white powder.

"What is it?"

"Coke, man."

"I don't have that kind of money."

Kurt threw the vial at Corelli's chest. "My going away present. Just be careful with that shit."

"I can't take this."

"Yeah, you can. Don't sweat it."

Putting on his jacket, he threw one duffle bag over each shoulder and grabbed an envelope from the top of his dresser. "Give this to Jules for me?"

"Sure. And thanks."

The young man paused. His blue eyes took on a dark hue, reflecting his own tragedies, "I once witnessed a guy hallucinating because of that stuff. Thought there were insects crawling under his skin. He took a potato peeler to his arm, to get them out. You don't want nightmares like mine. Trust me."

They shook hands. Corelli watched as Kurt left the boarding house, leaving a vacancy that extended past the fabric of an empty room.

"I already have them," he said to no one.

[141]

~

Her legs encircled his waist as he held her against the wall, bodies glistening with sweat, moving as if possessed by a preternatural force. Aroused by a chemical stimulant, she awoke from her state of lethargy feeling an insatiable sexual hunger. He kissed her wine-stained lips, tasting forbidden fruit on his tongue. Her nails dug into his flesh as he penetrated her, attempting to reach the most sacred part of her. Carrying her to the bed, he hovered over her like a protective field, basking in her release as she orgasmed. Their animas mingled, colliding, forever conjoined. Taking his head in her hands, she asked him without words to explore her body; to stimulate her orally, allowing her to leave behind the mind-numbing sorrow that engulfed her. He strayed from his God; further, further. In his mind, the page was no longer blank, but filled with her name. Darkness washed over them, born of a night sky; black, like the magic that enwrapped them.

~

They reveled in a state of self-induced languor. The air was heavy as proclamations of love lingered, never spoken. Things scathing were obliterated with every touch. He watched as she rose from bed, her svelte form drifting.

[142]

The light of a silvery moon filtered through his window. Iridescence bounced off the glass in his mother's frame, bringing the woman to life. She emerged from it, healthy and young. Jules' voice sent her back inside.

"Where are they?"

"What, baby? What are you looking for?"

"Your army greens. I know this is where I put them," she said, rifling through his drawers. "Come on, come on...out, out, sprout, sprout."

He paled, unable to comprehend her incantation.

"You mean, your dad's army greens?"

"I found them," she said, holding up a pair of Corelli's Levi's. She rubbed at them furiously. "I don't know if the blood will come out. *Dammit."*

"Jules."

She stared at him innocently, "What?"

"Come back to bed."

She dropped his pants to the floor, but she stood frozen in place, her feet cemented to the hardwood.

"Who is that?" she asked, pointing across the room.

He tried to focus through a purple haze. Shadowy figures came to life, like a desert mirage, and retreated into their sordid dens.

"There's no one here but us. It's only your shadow."

"Oh."

She approached him, exuding sensuality, her stare, provocative. Beneath the covers, she ran her hand between his thighs, teasing him with her lascivious ways. She straddled him and leaned in close; her breasts warm against his chest. *"Why did I have a wine stem in my eye?"* she whispered.

"I pull her into me, so close, feeling her soft skin beneath my burning fingers. She lets herself succumb to me, unafraid of my wicked love. Our bodies perish, simultaneously spent, and we begin our descent home to hell."

-Cris Corelli's Diary, October 19th, 1985

Sixteen

His bare feet left imprints on the hardwood. The noon day sun was offensive. Cloaked in darkness, he was able to drop the charade. On her breath, his Christian name took on new meaning. She breathed life into him, reaching out to him from the equinox that divided their hearts. She was his drug.

As his eyes darted across empty rooms, he called out to her, hearing only his echo. Panic lodged itself in his throat. Ghosts withdrew, afraid of the sunlight. Memories infiltrated through the cracks in the window coverings. He saw himself driving without any sense of direction, cursing, and pounding at the steering wheel of her new car. His mother had a habit of disappearing after every argument. He had found her, finally, sitting on a park swing with her cane between her feeble legs, mumbling a soliloquy to her audience of pigeons. It was then that he first learned of her disease.

Aromas were non-existent as he entered the kitchen. The kettle, cold. The stove, turned off.

"Goddamnit, where the fuck are you?"

He jerked his head towards the foyer at the sound of the front door closing. Hurrying through the Great Room, he found her in her office, sitting on the couch, holding something to her chest.

"Where did you go?" He scratched at his naked abs. A deep chill ran up his spine, foreshadowing what was to come.

"Corelli. Come closer."

He sat next to her, eyeing the blanket that she held to her breast. His insides churned, as he revisited the night's horrors in his mind.

"I was worried. When did you get up?"

"Early. This little one couldn't wait."

Pulling the pink coverlet down, her face glowing, she revealed a doll. Its plastic lips suckled on her dry nipple.

"Jesus fucking Christ," he whispered, coming to his feet. His hand met his mouth as he came to the realization that she was in the place where grieving mothers go: Hell's Waiting Room.

"It's a girl. Just like I wanted!"

"Jules…"

"What's wrong? Don't be scared, Corelli. All new fathers are. You'll get over it. Do you want to hold her?" she asked, pushing the toy in his direction.

He held his hand out -- to stave off the devil. "Jules, did you…did you do it this morning? Without me?"

"Do what?" She nestled the fake baby in her arm. Tears of joy spilled onto its plastic face. "Isn't she perfect?" she asked gazing up at him.

[147]

Her features fell as he turned away in repugnance. His back to her, he racked his brain, searching for the right words, but there were none that could appease an unsound mind. He thought of the penitent, seeking absolution, and the way he used to extricate their suffering by reciting lines from folk tales. He was a fraud then. He is a fraud now.

Slowly, he turned on his heel to see her rocking a pretend child. Demons were huddled around her; their fangs dripped scarlet ichor in anticipation.

"Did you name her?" he asked, choking on the question. He looked away, desperate not to cry.

"Not yet. I wanted to do that with you."

"I...I'd be honoured," he said, facing her. "Come on. Bring her upstairs."

"Okay."

The three of them made their way towards the spiral staircase. Jules walked ahead of him with the doll over her shoulder. Baby's perpetual smile made him want to gouge his eyes out. Her petrified arms were raised above her head in greeting. He waved back, like any good father should.

"We had a funeral today. I dug a hole six feet under. It's ironic that we place the dearly departed closer to Satan, and hope they find their way up."

-Cris Corelli's Diary

Seventeen

I'm sorry to put you out, kid. If you're reading this, my time has come. I'm alone in this world. You may not know it, but I was married once upon a time. Clarissa went ahead without me more than thirty years ago. She was on a plane, on her way home to me, when it crashed in the South Pacific. I miss her. I'm on my way to see her. This here boarding house has been my home. I want to be buried here. I know Lissa won't mind. She always said that it won't matter if we're apart physically. God wants our souls. There's a spot by the old shack where I like to go and think about life. With each sunset, I revisit a chapter in my life. You'll know the place. If you can set my banjo in there with me, I'd truly appreciate it. I always said I'd like to have her listen to me play. Couldn't play a thing before she died. Had to fill the holes in my heart somehow. Bury me in my brown suit and red polka-dot bow tie. I married her in that suit. Don't want no flowers. Lissa is allergic to them. Anyway, I bet you hope I put the meaning of life at the end of this letter. Truth is, I don't know what it is. There is one thing I do know for sure, though. Love is the only thing that matters. The world is a cold, ugly, place without it.

Truly Yours, Ol' Mike Wilkinson.

Trees were barren. Their skeletal remains were indicative of a muted Autumn. In the distance, a farmer's plow competed with the eternal pounding recurring in Corelli's head. He had dragged the man's body down the stairs and into a wheelbarrow, likening the funeral procession to a comedy of errors.

Jules' token tears watered the freshly dug soil. Corelli refused to deliver a eulogy for the old man. Instead, she softly spoke a childhood prayer in Mike's honour.

Now I lay me down to sleep,
I pray the Lord, my soul to keep,
If I should die before I wake,
I pray the Lord my soul to take.

"How are we going to mark the grave?"

"I'll build something tomorrow. Let's go. It's getting cold out."

"Especially for Cristina," Jules said, staring down at the baby sling crossing her chest.

Corelli bit the inside of his cheek, savouring the blood. He imagined tearing the ridiculous thing from her body and burying it with Mike. Leaving his shovel at the head of the grave, he bid the old man good-bye in his native tongue, *"Vai con Dio."*

"What's that mean?"

[151]

"It means, 'Go with God'."

"I thought you were mad at Him."

"Force of habit. Come on," he said, guiding her towards the boarding house.

"No. I'm not going. Not until you tell me why you're mad at Him."

He saw his mother standing beside her wearing Shakespearean garb. Her shriveled face was covered in tumors, and as her casket emerged from the earth, inviting him inside, misery gave way to anger.

"Do you want to know why I left the priesthood?"

"Yeah," she said, adopting an ordinary expression, "I do."

"I fucking left because He let her die. I left because He let me..."

"Let you? Let you, *what?* And don't swear in front of the baby!"

Expletives befouled the air between them.

"It's a fucking doll, Jules! Wake the *fuck* up!"

"I'm going to forgive you for that, Corelli," she said, dangerously close to losing her mind. "Only once."

"You have to wake up, Jules," he said, imploring her. "It's the Coke. Your grief..."

"Once," she repeated, walking away from him.

He brought the flashlight to life and caught up to her. Beneath its glare, she looked like she could crumble, like

[152]

the victims of Pompeii, immortalized in ash. "I'm sorry," he said, "but you have to listen to me."

Covering her ears with her hands, she ran, stumbling her way back home, where the ghosts were waiting; phantasms with familiar names.

"Christ!"

A cigarette met his lips. He exhaled all the impure and polluted thoughts that swirled around his brain. As she grew tinier, so did his courage. Extinguishing the flashlight, he walked blind, feeling comforted by the dark; his sins, obscured. Halfway back to the boarding house, he tripped and met the ground. He stayed there, his face in the cold grass, imagining what it would be like to meet his Maker.

Sitting up, he rubbed the dirt from his hands. He heard rosary beads rattle in his ears. He hit himself in the head, over, and over, but the rattling would not stop. He wrapped his arms around his knees and stared at the celestial ocean above him. Humbled by his love for her, he sought help from the One he no longer believed in, "God, please. I know You don't want to hear from me, but You have to help us, Lord."

The wind blew fierce. There was no answer coming from the heavens. Surrendering, he placed his hands beside him to raise himself up. The stone beneath his hand felt foreign. He shone the flashlight on it and squinted to make out the words that were weathered by time and the earth's elements: "ane" , "923".

Crawling on his hands and knees he searched the area around him. He came across a second stone, buried beneath a pile of rotting leaves, and like the pieces of a puzzle, he fit the two together: "Chrane. 1890-1923."

He stared at the marker for a long time, trying to make sense of it. Memories of things past were like pinpricks on his brain. He stood facing the boarding house, that seemed to breathe, expanding, and contracting like a living entity. Walking slowly towards it, he saw a cross materialize on the highest peak. He jogged closer to it, scanning it with eyes wide, unwilling to believe in the grotesque. The windows were boarded, concealing something that man did not want seen. He ran until he reached the front door and frantically searched the area, fingers running over brick, feeling each crack and crevice, reading it like a blind man does Braille. Beneath the simple wooden sign, he could see a hint of bronze – a plaque of some sort in commemoration or memoriam. Swinging the front door open, he stood at the threshold of the Great Room and saw pews in the expansive space holding sinners who bowed their heads in shame. The giant hearth was now an altar, where Christ's blood ran from the sacred chalice, and above it, a man hung from a cross – a man who looked just like he did.

The devil had come to play.

[154]

He backed away slowly, gagging on his saliva as he said the words in haste, *"Dear God."*

In her office, he found her toolbox.

"What are you doing?"

She had entered the room, unseen. The long, black, silk slip she wore hugged her curves. An open bottle of wine was clutched in her hand; her eerie smile, ever-present.

Ignoring her, he pushed past her and stood on the front porch with a screwdriver and a hammer poised underneath the wooden sign. Her presence filled the doorway.

"What are you *doing!?*"

"Go back inside, Jules."

"I won't."

He dropped the tools at his feet and grasped her by her upper arms, meeting her eyes with an intensity he reserved for morticians, and the devil himself, "I need you to go inside and wait for me," he said, enunciating every syllable. Kissing her on the forehead, he pushed her across the threshold and closed the door.

Saintly riddles enticed him. Picking up the tools, he jammed the screwdriver beneath the wood and used the hammer to pull at the makeshift sign. It fell to the ground with a thud, revealing the unconscionable truth.

St. Anthony's Parish

1912

In the Glory of God

Blessed by Reverend Thomas. R. Neeland

Stumbling down the stairs, he dropped to his knees. *"Fuck. Fuck."* He heard shrieking on the wind, high-pitched cries uttering his name. Scrambling to his feet, he ran up the steps and into the boarding house, securing the lock. His head met the door. His laboured breathing was audible.

"You're acting awfully strange."

He spun around to see her standing there, waiting. With the tools still clutched in his hands, he ran past her, into the Great Room, and dragged a table up against the wall. He worked, trying to remove the shutter from the window. Sweat pooled at the nape of his neck.

"Stop that, Corelli."

He looked down at her with twisted features, unable to focus on her angelic face. The hammer met the shutter and he pounded at it, defacing it, his muscles burning from the strain.

"I said, stop that."

He was deaf to her words. The shutter gave way, and he tossed it to the side. One of the Stations of the Cross was in full view, its colours rich and vibrant, depicting Veronica wiping Jesus' disfigured face. The window dripped with the blood of the Redeemer. He wiped at it and stared at his hand, clean -- soiled only by his wickedness.

"What is going *on!?*"

Her crying competed with the voices that grew louder, otherworldly groans berating him for his stupidity.

"We're in a Church," he said, laughing hysterically. "We're in a *fucking* Church."

"Oh, God…"

The wine bottle crashed to the floor. Her hand instinctively met her crucifix. She clutched at it, seeking comfort. Corelli jumped from the table and stood before her, grasping her head in his hands. The apology spilled from his lips, "I'm sorry, Jules. I'm sorry for ever stopping here. I'm…sorry for loving you so damn much."

"What are you saying?" she asked, suddenly lucid. "You're scaring me, Corelli."

Dropping his hands, he turned from her. An odor filled his nostrils. Hypnotized by the stench, he approached the kitchen, lungs burning. Inside the oven, Cristina was slowly melting; her cherubic face distorting into something demonic.

"Jesus."

"I didn't mean to," Jules said. "Are you mad?" she asked, walking towards him.

He raised his hands as if to box with the devil, making her recoil in fear. Reaching out to her, he embraced

[157]

her, evicting Satan as he tried to overtake her body. He kissed her eyes, her neck, her forehead, where her sickness ran deep – infecting her beautiful mind.

"I belong here," he whispered in her hair.

She trembled beneath him; her lungs starved for air. Nodding, she quietly begged God for mercy.

"I'm not leaving you, Corelli," she said, meeting his eyes. "I need you here. With me. Remember? Because I do. I fucking remember, Corelli."

He kissed her, hard.

Releasing her, he walked to the other side of the steel table, putting a barrier between them. He gazed at her with tremendous adoration. There were vows yet to keep, and a final kiss to be had. His senses were drowned in her. The world became untainted. Heaven was no longer a mystical concept. It was the tone of her voice, the feel of her lips on his, and the sweet, delicious, torture of pure love.

"I love you, Jules."

He opened a drawer beneath him and walked back towards her with a towel in his hand. With her by his side, he switched on the gas burner, torching the rag, and lighting things ablaze.

Enthralled by the rousing fire, they felt a divine force envelop them. Sins were purged. Forgiveness, granted.

"Don't be afraid," he said, taking her hand.

They walked to the Great Room, where sermons

were once spoken, and confessions were heard, and it was there that they would find everlasting peace.

She stared up at him with the eyes of a child, pure, wholesome, and as flames danced around them, she spoke the words that he would take to his fiery grave, "Will you love me tomorrow?"

Amen.

Books by Barbara Avon

Peter Travis Love Stories:

My Love is Deep

Briana's Bistro

The Christmas Ornament

The Christmas Miracle

A Two-Part Love/Time Travel Story:

Promise Me

Romance/Suspense/Time Travel:

STATIC

Timepiece

Windfall

Romance/Thriller:

The Gift

Michael's Choice

Horror:

The Simpleton
SPEED BUMP

Psychological Horror/Thriller:

Sacrilege

Paranormal Romance:

Postscript
Q.W.E.R.T.Y.

A Collection of Flash Fiction:

Love Bites
Love Still Bites

About the Author

Barbara Avon was born in Switzerland and immigrated to Canada when she was two years old. She grew up Italian in the Niagara Region and attended Notre Dame High School, and then Brock University. She moved to Ottawa, Ontario, in 1999 to pursue work. She has worked for two major Ottawa area magazines and is a published poet.

Always having had a penchant for the written word, she has dreamed of writing a novel. "Sacrilege", is her sixteenth. She is also the author of three unique children's books that allow the child to draw the illustrations, and a compilation of micro-fiction, "Love Bites." She is working on her next novel, a love story with her characteristic suspense element.

In 2018, she won SpillWords Author of the Month, as well as FACES Magazine "Favourite Female Author". She is an active member of the Writing Community on Twitter (@barb_avon).

Together with her husband, she has established BUCCILLI Publishing in homage to her maiden name.

Avon lives in Ontario, Canada with her husband Danny, their tarantula Betsy, and their houseplant, "Romeo".

Printed in Great Britain
by Amazon